SONG OF THE EXECUTION

Lisa Talbott

Lineage Independent Publishing
Marriottsville, MD

ISBN (paperback): 9781958418154
First Released in the United Kingdom

Publisher: Lineage Independent Publishing, Marriottsville, MD

Maryland Sales and Use Tax Entity: Lineage Independent Publishing, Marriottsville, MD 21104

Contact: hurdmp@lineage-indypub.com

Website: https://lineage-indypub.com

"Death by lethal injection" were the four most terrifying words Trevor Brown ever heard in the eighteen years of his young life. It numbed his whole being, so much so that he was unable to hear anything afterwards.

He'd always professed to be afraid of nothing. But now he was! He feared every minute and hour of every single day that the ticking clock stole from him.

Contents

Foreword

Once again, I am honored to be the editor and publisher of a Lisa Talbott novel. It seems like only yesterday that Lisa and I were exchanging "what ifs" in social media chat sessions. In the four years since that initial contact, our relationship has grown into a true friendship.

"Song of the Execution" brings Lisa's formidable talent to bear on a societal issue: wrongful convictions of Black men in the United States. Though fiction, this novel could have been any Black man's story in real life. Wrong place, wrong time, perhaps? You'll just have to read the story and draw your own conclusions.

Regardless of the societal issues, Lisa should be applauded for taking on such a daunting story line. The United States legal system is fraught with twists and turns: she navigates through them as if she had first-hand knowledge (thankfully, she hasn't!). As I read and edited the story, I was amazed at the visual images Lisa was able to paint and could visualize the events as though I were there in the room with the characters. I should note that Lisa has never been in the United

States; rather, she is a British subject who has retired to the hinterlands of Portugal, "at the end of the Internet," as I often tease.

I am sure that you will enjoy this book as much as I did! And... watch out for a few twists and turns!

Michael Paul Hurd
Author/Editor/Publisher
Lineage Independent Publishing

1: In Court

Trevor Carlton Brown stood in the dock awaiting his sentence to be announced. He was feeling dizzy, his heart thumping ten to the dozen in his chest, his limbs trembling nervously while his hands and body felt clammy with fear and dread.

He managed to glance surreptitiously over to his mother who had never taken her eyes off him. She was sitting with Eva, his younger sister. He would have sold his soul to the devil to have avoided putting his family through this enormously unfair charade. Trevor felt his mother had aged in the six months since he'd been incarcerated. Her usually cheery smile had been replaced with an aura of shame and disbelief. He broke eye contact, trying to concentrate on the proceedings whilst at the same time imagining himself far, far away.

The court room was filled with onlookers, 'sticky beakers', predators lying in wait to hear his sentence. Those who would possibly be spending the rest of the day rejoicing and celebrating alongside those others who would therein-after be filled with despair, never to be the same again… depending on the outcome of the next few minutes.

The courtroom was a magnificent building to behold with its light oak panelled walls, rows of seats, beamed ceilings, and huge arched windows that the afternoon sun poured its rays through, reminding everyone that normal life continued outside, regardless.

Not a sound could be heard, bar the odd whispers, coughs, and ticking of the huge clock above the judge's podium. Its tick-tick-ticking, seeming deafeningly louder each time the second hand moved menacingly forward.

Trevor stared at the clock as it mockingly continued its purpose, wishing he could stride over and move the hands back - weeks, months… He had wished for the same scenario every day that he'd been held in custody whilst awaiting his trial.

Judge Turpin, attired in the traditional black gown, entered the courtroom and sat sternly at his podium; a scraping of his chair as he drew closer to read the papers in front of him made everyone sit up straight and hold their breath. The jury had already rendered their verdict. It was now all up to Judge Turpin to deliver the outcome.

His death sentence was read out as though it was a mere formality, akin to an announcement that one could expect to hear over the public address system at a train station. A voice that lacked any sorrow belonging to a face that showed anything other than relief to eventually call it a day.

The words thudded in his ears and seemed to float before his eyes, and he couldn't understand it. He clearly heard his mother's disbelieving sob amidst the cheers and stomping of feet in the auditorium then watched her head drop to her knees. He was aware of the banging of the gavel as the judge called out for order.

Trevor Carlton Brown was only eighteen years old and had no idea if he would ever see his nineteenth birthday as he was handcuffed and led away by two burly uniformed security officers. The brand-new black suit and shoes he wore, were, he acknowledged, a waste of his mother's hard-earned money as it was obvious they would never again see the light of day.

"I wish I could write something that would last for an eternity."

"Everything you write *will* last for an eternity, for it will be written."

"I mean, I wish it would be profound, significant, and people would never forget me."

"Ah… I see. But not everything lasts within our memory for ever. It is only with reading again or revisiting that reminds us. That is why it's important for you to continue writing, to immortalise your memories for others to read and share your experiences."

"But what if it seems boring, uninteresting?"

"Then so be it! We all have different tastes and stories to tell. You will never please everybody, nor should you wish to, because then your words *will* be boring to some readers."

"But I don't want to be forgotten. I don't just want to be a number either. My name is Trevor Brown, I'm not just 8356. I shouldn't be here, it's all a big mistake and nobody listened to me…"

"Trevor Brown, 8356, then listen to me and forget that nobody listened to you, because they're certainly not hearing you now. Deaf ears will never hear things they're not willing to listen to. They just want the joy of probability to overtake the perception of doubt. You get my drift, boy? History hasn't moved so much since your great-grandfather's era. You were found guilty because of the evidence stacked against you by those so-called experts. Same as now. You could have tried convincing that jury that the sun is yellow but if they say it's green, the masses will all agree that that big ball of fire in the skies, is indeed green. Get over it."

"But I'm scared, Cole."

Cole was silent. He heard that familiar tremor in Trevor's voice and remembered a similar conversation he'd had years ago with Bud Rogers before he even thought of writing his song for his execution.

He was probably double the age of Trevor Brown 8356 at the time, and Bud Rogers was sixty-two. His moment had arrived, time to pay his dues.

There was no mistaking the procedure, the condemned knowing well ahead of the others in 'the club' and then the tantalising smells of food permeating the corridor as if to taunt all, reminding them of what normality lay beyond their existence.

Of course it was purgatory for everyone else. They salivated as the specialised food was wheeled to the cell of the prisoner who was being given his last meal. Those aromas were a reminder of what was to come when *their* day arrived.

Cole remembered hearing the pitiful glee from Rogers upon seeing the vast array of delicacies. He heard his grunts as he devoured the last food to touch his lips before he was taken to the room with the electric chair, and he remembered the words he spoke prior to his departure amidst his fervour to enjoy his last meal: "I'm scared, man."

But Bud Rogers was not as cultured or personable as Trevor Brown, and truly deserved his awaiting fate. He had an exuberant audience of over a hundred, eagerly anticipating watching his body shudder and violently shake, that would whoop and cheer when it was all over.

"Fear can be seen as a sign of weakness, kid. You're here in 'the club' same as us all. You felt brave enough to do what you did to put you here in the first place, why you telling me you scared?"

"You're right, you're right. I suppose you would think I deserve to be here, in 'the club', but I'm worried you see. I'm beginning to think I'm not as brave as I thought I was. I hate being afraid of the pain I know I'm going to suffer."

Cole knew exactly what he meant, they all did, but not one of them would admit to it out loud, especially to another 'clubber'. "You might strike lucky and actually be given a sedative, but don't count on it. They like to withhold this little privilege. It all adds to their version of 'fun'. Just another sin of executioners".

The lights went out in the cells and everywhere was once again in the same familiar darkness, leaving Trevor with even more questions he needed answers to.

The routines were as regimental as the breaking of the dawn the next mornings. Each man contemplating how he was going to pass the hours away until sleep prevailed, hoping that dreams of past lives overtook the dark and lonely hours. Dreams of teenage years and family Christmases, school days and school friends before being rightly or wrongly in the predicament they were now in.

"Sleep tight, kid. Don't let the bed bugs bite."

3: Trevor Carlton Brown – The Early Years

"Mom, when I grow old, can I be an astronaut and fly to the moon, like Buzz Aldrin or Neil Armstrong?"

Trevor was sitting with his mother on their front porch, looking up at the stars. He was eight years old and was fascinated with astronomy and space travel. He'd watched everything on the television related to those sciences, yearning for the day he would encounter a UFO, convinced he would someday have the unique opportunity to encounter species from another planet.

"Son, you can be whatever you wish to be, but that means you have to work hard at school and do your homework every night like your teacher tells ya. Only you decides which road you gonna take."

Trevor didn't like the reasoning of his mother's reply. He didn't see the point in doing his homework after school, because of course school was where he was supposed to learn everything. He hated homework, much preferring to run outside and join his friends, playing. He couldn't understand why he needed to sit down and do the task the teacher had assigned when he could quite simply copy from a classmate. Clearly, his mother had no understanding of how already brilliant he was!

School, he considered, was a place where only the very young people had to go to learn, like Eva, his younger sister. And all girls, too, because girls didn't know things that boys knew. Trevor watched television: everything he needed to learn was right there on the television screen and it was fascinating.

He'd watch everything from documentaries to films. A whole wealth of knowledge was there at the click of a remote control and therefore school was pointless. It was a waste of his time and his mother's money to buy a uniform when he could sit at home and learn the wonders of the world in his own time and from a comfortable settee.

"Homework is a punishment, Mama. It only justifies the teacher's workload. Why do I have to write an essay on something I have no interest in when I could be watching something educational on the television? If I watch enough space programmes I can be an astronaut and land on the moon and then I can write a book about my experiences. I can be famous and then you wouldn't have to work at the store and grow vegetables in the garden or make clothes for me and Eva cos I'd be rich and you could buy anything you wanted to."

Anne raised her eyebrows in surprise and humour. "What, Son?" she laughed, "you don't think we rich already? Don't you have clothes on your back and boots on your feet? A roof over your head and food in your belly? Do you think we poor? I thought I just heard you say that television teaches you everything you need to know, evidently you not been listening hard enough, hence you've made it abundantly obvious why you should do your darned homework and get yourself educated."

"Trevor, don't for one minute think you know it all because you know nothing, boy. You eight years old. Did you know your great-granddaddy was born on a plantation, he never was privileged to have an education like me and you, he had to work hard all day long and…"

Trevor switched off, rolling his eyes. He'd heard the stories ad nauseum from his mother, his grandmother and his aunt since as far back as he could remember. He hated hearing those accounts of the 'olden days', he wasn't interested in the past, he was too focussed on the future, his bright future!

He left his mother sitting on the porch to reminisce, reliving the nostalgia of her formative years, confident in his naive immaturity to know where his destiny was heading.

4: Jonah

Jonah Ray was 23 years old: still single, still living on the farm and looking after his bed-ridden mother. Almost six feet tall, not overly good-looking, but muscled and incredibly strong. He was lighter skinned than either of his Afro-Caribbean parents had been, which had caused his father to doubt his true paternity even though his wife, Sadie, had sworn her faithfulness time and time again: but as Jonah grew, so did the rift between father and son as Raymond failed to acknowledge any resemblance to himself or forefathers whatsoever.

When Jonah's father, Raymond Ray, died that summer nine years previously after being bitten by a rattle snake while clearing a piece of land ready to plant a crop of sweet corn, Jonah was beside himself with grief. He'd always yearned for his father's love and approval, a constant at his beck and call, assisting, fetching, carrying, waiting to earn a smile and thank you.

At thirteen years old, the farmstead was up to him to manage, and school was out of the question. There was no way his mother could afford his time away now that Raymond had gone. It was all going to end up on young Jonah's shoulders.

He was harbouring two lines of thoughts in this regard. He knew what needed to be done because he'd watched and helped his father for years, so it was simply a matter of continuation. It was second nature to him to feed the chickens, work the land, set the potatoes, corn, and the pumpkins, harvest the yield. He enjoyed the initial responsibility of becoming the breadwinner and the reason for his and his mother's survival.

The other train of thought was more of a disappointing route he was going to be undertaking because he would miss the camaraderie of his school chums, the socialising, the after-school sports activities like basketball he enjoyed, and of course the chance of seeing Anne Brown every day.

He'd been sweet on Anne ever since their early school days, but she had barely given him a second glance, until that afternoon she was stung by a bee.

The children were sitting at their desks in class and the teacher writing mathematical questions on the blackboard. Suddenly a huge grey cloud hovered outside the open window, causing everyone to look up and wonder what was happening outside. Very slowly, almost in silence, the cloud entered through the open window, and everyone panicked, rushing out from their seats screaming out loud, and wildly swatting their arms above their heads.

Jonah was the only one who remained seated and calm - beside his teacher - because he knew that the bees were just looking for an alternative home. He sat mesmerised, observing in awe for several minutes before standing up and slowly walking towards the door to let the bees continue their journey outside.

One or two of the children were stung, and Jonah explained to his hysterical classmates that if only they'd remained calm, the bees wouldn't have hurt anyone. He took Anne's arm and chastised her for her stupidity.

"You need to get home and put some baking soda and tooth paste on the sting, or even some of your mom's apple cider vinegar. The bees would never have reacted aggressively if you'd left them alone. They were with their queen, looking for a new home. Did you know that if all the bees died, then we would die, too. We need all the bees to pollinate everything we eat."

Anne was indignant. "What rubbish you speak Jonah Ray, they most certainly do not pollinate chickens, or cows!"

Before he could enlighten her, the teacher intervened. "Jonah is right, Anne, the bees were just trying to find somewhere to make a new hive. They don't react at all unless they feel threatened, which is what some of them must have felt by everyone's hysteria, hence you've all learned a valuable lesson today, wouldn't you agree?"

The teacher continued, "You should never kill the bees; they are a lifeline to all human beings. Without them we would have no fruits on our trees, no vegetables growing in our gardens. We should respect them as much as we should respect every living creature on our little planet."

That was the day that Anne really had any liaison with Jonah, it was also the day he decided he was going to become a beekeeper. He was eventually going to do something to garner admiration from his father by building a couple of beehives, to ensure they get the best crops around. He was going to stand out from his peers too, because they were all scaredy cats whilst he'd been brave and weathered the storm, or the swarm!

He got three books from the library the very next day on 'Beekeeping'. He was excited!

"Eva. Eva, wake up! Sshhh! Don't talk, Mom's sleeping, don't wake her up!"

Eva stirred, alarmed, wondering why her brother was waking her from her sleep.

"What, Trevor, what's wrong?"

"Nothing's wrong, I just gotta go pop out for a short while that's all. I forgot something and I'm gonna need to climb out of your window and back in again so don't put the latch on! I can't use the back door cos she'll hear me, so just go back to sleep and forget you've seen me, okay? And don't be scared when you hear me come back. I'll only be gone just a few minutes."

Eva looked at her bedside clock, it was almost midnight. In her slumber she was unable to comprehend why her brother needed to climb out of her bedroom and then come back again, for something he'd forgotten to do?

"Why can't you wait until the morning? What's so important that you have to go now, at this time of night, Trevor? Please don't ask me to lie and cover for you because if Mom finds out we'll both be in trouble and that's not fair on me. No. I'm not doing it, go back to bed and sort it out tomorrow."

"Eva, don't give me grief, I've told you I'll only be gone a few minutes. It can't wait until tomorrow, I have to go now and all I'm asking you to do is not lock the window so that I can get back in, that's all. Mom doesn't need to know, so shut up whinging. I'll lock the window when I come back, okay?"

"I don't like leaving the window unlocked. Mom tells me to keep it locked when I'm in bed. Where are you going?"

Trevor was getting agitated, "I'm going to see a man about a dog. You'll not even notice I've been gone."

And with that, he climbed out of Eva's bedroom window and thudded upon his landing outside.

6: Earl Ryder

Fifteen years Earl had worked at the prison, five as 'The Executioner'; a status of which he was now proud. His job had provided a very comfortable lifestyle for him and his wife, but it also brought him a huge amount of shame and embarrassment, never fully disclosing his true job description to his immediate family.

He would never forget the first time, how could he? Indeed, how would anyone forget their first time? He'd been assisting in executions by electric chair for many years before he took over full responsibility for the dastardly deed! It had been a Tuesday night and the 49ers game was being played live on TV, of which he was an ardent fan, having played for them for two months in his heyday, once-upon-a-time. He'd had to step into the shoes of the usual resident 'executioner' who was in hospital with a burst appendix, Lord knows if he was gonna survive!

Bud Rogers had been served his last meal, the one he'd requested, and the one that had everyone else on death row salivating as it was wheeled to his cell. Bud had permission to request any food he wanted, and he took great advantage of that. He wanted to go out on a bursting stomach, courtesy of the penitentiary funds.

He had a steak pie with mashed potatoes, corn, gravy and cornbread, a favourite meal his mother cooked when he was a boy. A medium-sized lobster sat on a side dish surrounded by lettuce, cherry tomatoes, and a slice of lemon. Apple strudel with ice cream for dessert, a harmonica, and a Bible.

Earl was always surprised when a 'clubber' requested a Bible. Were there words of comfort to be found inside that could make the condemned find some kind of peace after all? Were they looking for a way to absolve themselves in the scriptures?

He knew that Bud Rogers warranted what was coming to him and didn't deserve the luxury of the food that had been specially prepared. Horse shit was too good for the likes of him, and Earl would have been happy to have served it to him.

He used to kinda waltz down the aisle, smiling and whistling as he pushed the trolley of culinary delights, and often took great satisfaction in coughing up a gob full of phlegm to spit into the food that the condemned man was going to eat. He thought it was funny, robbing them of their final moments of dignity.

He also knew that the aromatic smells of food would tantalise the taste buds of the whole of death row inmates, which he relished, knowing they all deserved to be tortured this way.

He'd witnessed a fair few executions over the years but this time HE was going to be the sole executioner, the one who strapped the man down, watched the veins in his neck pulsating with fear, sniggering at seeing a grown man piss himself when his trousers showed the telltale sign of wetness, spreading like a coward's rash.

He would stare at his victim, the first time of becoming a bona fide murderer himself as he was about to pull the lever and endeavoured to remember his last words so that he was able to relay it to family members who actually did give a damn. He did, of course. Relishing in adding his own untrue version of events, telling them how they pleaded to God and cried pathetically for forgiveness.

He remembered that day, it was permanently embedded in his memory bank. Forever intruding in his dreams at night.

He heard the pathetic mumblings of "Earl, I'm scared man. Make it quick and painless, will you?"

Earl looked out to the audience of over a hundred strong. Bud Rogers' victims' families. Scavengers in disguise as law-abiding citizens because they were not wishing to 'turn the other cheek', they were there to witness someone else doing what they would love to do themselves, without any recourse. A matter of 'passing the buck?' Their hands and consciences squeaky clean.

He was strapped up. Possibly tighter than he should have been, but who was to care? He'd been given the obligatory condemned-man's sedatives to calm him before the procedure, never taking his eyes off Ryder. "Tell them I was good to go, man. You'll do that last thing for me, won't you? And can you... will you tell them I'm sorry?"

It was but a few minutes as Bud Rogers' body buckled and convulsed as the power surged through him, he shook, and emitted sounds that would haunt any decent human being till eternity. Through the glass screen, Earl watched as everyone moved closer to get a better view of the man they despised, their smiles spreading like a cheap margarine.

When it seemed as if the whole pantomime was over, the crowd beyond the glass dispersed, seemingly satiated. Now they could all go home and put the past behind them, raise a glass to toast to a job well done.

But not Earl. Not yet. When the doctor checked Bud's vitals to pronounce him dead, Earl was dismayed to hear a very faint beep on the monitor, which the doctor confirmed with his stethoscope. Earl knew another jolt of electricity was needed to finish the task and put Bud Rogers out of his misery with an ounce of dignity. Or should he?

As he debated carrying out the task, he looked into the agonised face of the abysmal rapist, paedophile, murderer, and vomited. He thought he was going to feel something of euphoria, satisfaction. After all, he'd felt privileged to have stepped up to the rank of executioner even if it was only to cover a colleague, but when the realisation set in, everything changed for Earl.

He'd just killed a man by his own actions, and he had no idea how he was to go home that night and sleep. He had always considered he was a law-abiding citizen; he was working to put a roof over his head, food on the table, but the words of Bud Rogers would haunt him every time he lay his head on his pillow:

"Earl. I'm scared man. Make it quick and painless will you?"

Did Bud Rogers hear the very same pitiful words from his victims? Did he care? Of course, he didn't; he was a coward as well as a lunatic who revelled in hearing the pleas and screams of all those he successfully tortured.

His execution should have been a joyous, momentous occasion to celebrate, crack open the champagne and rejoice at being 'the one' to rid society of such an evil being. And he had felt that way, with the others, when he was just 'assisting', but now another human-being had died due to *his* own actions and that made him feel that he himself somewhat deserved to be amongst the people he'd ridiculed for years.

He stood looking a while at the limp body of Bud Rogers and would attribute the shame of vomit on the floor to the dead man strapped in the purpose-built chair, dismissing the words of regret he'd heard that would never pass his lips. He would get over it.

7: Cole Cave

Cole leaned forward studying his reflection in the mirror above his sink, running his hands over his unshaven chin, fingering his facial lines that Father-Time had bestowed upon him, ageing him prematurely and wondering where the young handsome carefree man had disappeared to.

Of course, it wasn't a mirror per se, heaven forbid the prison issued such luxuries as a 'real' *glass* mirror which could be easily broken and used for all sorts of reasons, such as to cut one's wrists or use as a weapon to maim another inmate. No, that kind of thing wasn't allowed. Society didn't want to be denied the pleasure of a 'clubber' taking the easy road out by ending his own life.

Cole had always felt that they were now like gladiators, in the public eye, waiting to be thrown into the lion's den; a spectacle for the amusement of a blood-thirsty audience, like the bull fighting in some of the European countries.

What possessed people to pay to watch an innocent animal teased, speared, taunted, killed? The oh-so-brave matador attired in flamboyant costume playing to the whooping and cheering of a sadistic and barbaric audience?

That's what it was like, living on death row - or rather, *existing* on death row. A caged animal waiting for the circus ringmaster to crack the whip and dance to its tune for the pure enjoyment of perverted, wanting, spectators.

Cole Cave was coming up to his fiftieth year; ten of those behind bars. He started to notice white hairs mingling with the few remaining dark on his head, his chest, his eyebrows as he studied his reflection, trying to remember how it felt when he performed the task of shaving, combing his hair, splashing on the cologne before heading off to a bar or nightclub. Those blissful, carefree days when all he had to worry about was if he had enough money in his pocket to last the night, if he found an attractive young woman eager enough to let him buy her a drink, and perhaps a little more.

He stripped off his clothes in front of his sink and sighed, noticing that even his pubic hair was beginning to sprout white hairs, he was turning into an old man before he'd even had a chance to live as a young one.

Ten long years being incarcerated, locked up, banged up, whatever way you wish to call it, Cole was never gonna to enjoy that kind of liberation again, thanks to the lovely Carolyn . . or was that *Caroline*?

He was never going to watch a movie at the cinema surrounded by his crazy buddies, get drunk on Jamaican rum and coke after finishing work on a Friday night, nor ever imagine not being able to watch a pizza being made especially to his requirements. Those days were gone, only to be relived in a moments' lapse of self-pity. Cole Cave was now just a number, 5216, reduced as such in the same way as everyone else in 'the club', their identities replaced by mere digits in an environment where you were no longer classed as a human being!

Prison was home to them all. The guilty and the innocents, though most professed their innocence whilst even the innocent would claim to be guilty, basking in the glory of a crime they were far too much of a coward to have legitimately claimed notoriety. It stood them in good stead amongst their fellow inmates, keeping them at arm's length.

Cole had seen many 'numbers' being led away over the years. Some crying and begging, proclaiming their innocence, some walking upright, proud and silent, others dragged kicking and screaming.

The sound of the impending executions came in many guises, it usually depended on who was going to be the executioner.

They were all bastards in Cole's book. All of them sadistic murderers in their own right, relishing being involved in the procedure of a man taking his last breath, and truly deserved being behind the bars themselves. What was the difference for God's sake? Who decides the ultimate permission to decide right from wrong?

Executioner Hammond was the worst. Cole assumed he got his training in Auschwitz because he was without an ounce of empathy or compassion. All of the associated executioners were in a league of their own, they had to be, Ryder too. He knew the Hammonds and Ryders of the world. He knew because every man and woman on death row was the same. They were a league of like-minded souls.

8: Trevor

"Cole. How do you pass the time?"

"The same way as everyone passes the time here. Waiting, reflecting, breathing."

"For how long?"

"Huh? What do you mean 'for how long?', for the remainder of our time. Just the same as everyone else. There's nothing more we can do. We just get another day older, another year, just waiting… Boy, you're here because what you did is against the law and this is your punishment. This is all our punishment. There's no 'get out of jail' free card, you know. No Santa Claus to sit you on his knee and ask what you would like as a reward for being a good boy all year."

"I know, I know, but some folk do. Get out, I mean."

Cole laughed, a deep guttural laugh. "Are the words 'death by lethal injection' unclear to you boy? Did your lawyer not explain properly what you doing here?"

"But what if I were to apply for parole, because I can't be here just waiting until someone decides my time's up."

"That's exactly what you will be doing. Just like the rest of us, and then one day that 'someone' will have your name and number on a slip of paper with your expiry date written on, signed by the governor, issued to the press, and adieu, bon-voyage, cheerio old chap. You say you wanna write something memorable that folk will remember you by, yes?"

"Yes."

"It's not enough for you to know that you'll be remembered for the deed that put you here?"

"I don't want to be remembered for a wrong misdemeanour, Cole. I told you before, I shouldn't be here. I'm innocent."

"They don't think you innocent."

"I will write a book, I've decided. I'm going to write about how wrongly I've been treated, and when people read about me, they'll try to get me out of here, you'll see. And I'll get some compensation, too, because that's what happens, I've seen it all on the television. I'm still young, I have my whole life ahead of me, I have to be released."

Cole was exasperated, what was the kid thinking about? Did he really and truly think he didn't deserve to be where he was? Yes of course it had happened, once in a blue moon, but the jurisdictional system was much improved nowadays and rarely was an innocent person found guilty. The science was usually conclusive with the use of DNA, CCTV, the internet. One could hardly pass wind in this century without the whole world knowing. Technology could prove or disprove almost anything.

"That's a way to pass the time, writing, you might even be able to fill the library. Most folks here like a good comical read. I take it you gonna be writing fiction?" Cole sniggered.

"Fiction? No, no. I'm going to write my biography," the joke totally lost on him, "I had ambitions, I wanted to become an astronaut and write about my experiences. I was going to make my mother and sister proud of me, look after them. Who's going to do that while I'm cooped up in here?"

Cole's eyebrows raised in humour as he lay on his bunk, hands behind his head, forcing himself to listen to the ramblings of the voice next door, trying to picture this boy aspiring to the likes of Neil Armstrong wondering how the intellectual gene had managed to miss him!

"Oh boy, an astronaut, you say? That is one hell of an ambition. So… tell me, Trevor Brown, 8356, what prevented this monumental career path from becoming a reality for you?"

Trevor remained silent for a moment, considering his answer, "The universe was against me, I guess, but that doesn't mean the tide won't change to my advantage because I'm a big believer in that some things have to happen for a reason. Once my book is published, everyone will realise what they've done, what they're missing, and I can go home, start over again."

"I see. Well, good luck then. Ambition and hope are good. Oh, and by the way, don't forget that there are always two sides to every story!"

"And you, do you have ambition and hope?"

Cole sighed, heavily. *Was he ever gonna shut up?*

The lights went out and Cole looked upwards, watching the bulb lose its amber glow, Trevor's question playing with his thoughts.

Who didn't have ambitions and hope? Those were now feeble things to harbour considering their predicament. Indeed, it would be nice to still have ambition and hope but to what point? Ambition to see another birthday? Hope that their demise would be dignified and painless? Hope to wake up in the morning and finding the last despicable years were nothing more than a bad dream?

Wishing too, that's another word 'clubbers' wouldn't use in their vocabulary because wishing was excruciating. Wishing to turn the clocks back. Wishing to have been in a different place, or a different time. Wishing for the impossible, day after day after day.

"G'night, boy. Don't let the bed . . . "

"You didn't answer my question. You must have had ambitions and hopes. Everybody does."

"It doesn't matter, I'm here now. Perhaps in my next life I will achieve something, I'll do things differently. I will have paid my debt and the good Lord will see me right next time around. I guess my destiny was what He had in mind for me all along."

"But your mother, how did she take it? You know, you being here and condemned to die, and your family, how are…"

"I said good night, boy! Enough now."

Cole wanted to blot out the words he'd been subjected to hear. He wanted to stop the ringing in his ears, punch the narrator, kick his cell door open, run out into the open and never stop. He wanted to find a black hole that could transport back twenty-five years where he would find a rabbit hole, a cave surrounded by forests, mountains, rivers, where no other human being would ever find him and where he could inhale the scents of the fir trees, drink the deliciously freezing cold water from a spring. Somewhere warm where he wouldn't need clothes, and fertile ground to grow vegetables and fruits, where he could be at one with the animals. Somewhere like heaven.

"Damn and blast you, Carolyn!" (Neil Diamond's Sweet Caroline lyrics haunted him for the remainder of the night.)

"Cole Elijah Perkins, how do you plead?"

His eyes rapidly sought out Caroline, scanning the sea of scowling, venomous glares, willing her to offer him one last chance of a familiar smile. He then looked away, staring blankly into nowhere, "not guilty, your honour."

There was a loud mumbling in the courtroom, a heavy, despondent sigh from someone at the back, a momentary gasp of disbelief from Caroline. Her head bowed with a faint tear running down her cheek that she hoped the accused man wouldn't see. She would never forget this day, or that day, or indeed any day thereafter.

She watched a man she had known from years back, one she had befriended and laughed with, be taken down, manacled, emasculated, yet felt almost euphoric, indeed satiated. A slight tremor of remorse, guilt, shame? She would walk out of that courtroom on that hot summer day bearing the weight of the world on her young shoulders, totally aware that she had just signed his death warrant. She felt wretched, spent, but at the same time satisfied she had done what needed to be done. Justice had been served.

9: Anne Brown

Anne's second pregnancy with Eva was a doddle in comparison to Trevor, her first, having none of the dreaded nauseating morning sickness bouts, the inability to enjoy her first cup of tea, cravings to suck on lemons, or excruciating swollen and tender breasts. In fact it had been a surprise to discover the zip on her dress wouldn't perform one Sunday morning as she was readying herself for church and chastised herself for her obvious gluttony, resulting in the excess inches!

She panicked, hardly daring to acknowledge her thoughts, considering her missed periods. Her mother would be furious - again!

She recalled the first time, four years ago when she was just sixteen, her mother screaming blue murder at her, demanding to know who was responsible for leading her daughter astray, then isolating her from her younger sister should she lead her, too, onto the same path of debauchery.

Anne never told. It was too unthinkable and secretive to tell anyone, and it hadn't been as nice and exciting as he'd told her it would be. She was expecting something magical and fulfilling, as she had been chosen especially, allegedly.

Well, she had been 'filled' as was promised, and was getting fuller and fuller and had no reason to doubt the ordination she'd been assured, having no clue as to why her mother was in hysterics. Didn't the Sunday sermons extol the virtues of the Virgin Mary, mother to their worshipped and adored Jesus! Didn't the preachings extend to forgiveness, acceptance, and turning the other cheek? If the Virgin Mary was to be revered for the part she played in bearing a child two thousand years ago, a then unmarried young woman to boot, what was the difference now? At least Anne *knew* who the father of her child was, unlike Mary who apparently never declared it was Joseph! Had he forced her to lie, too? Had he told her the same story she'd been told, that it was God's will, and forced her to drink the same several glasses of wine before the unthinkable deed was done?

At sixteen years old, she was a stunner. Her black skin shone in the sunlight, as did her perfect pearly whites every time she laughed, which was often. Heads, male and female alike, would turn as she entered the church with her mother. Some out of admiration, some out of jealously, and others in lust.

An unmarried mother of two children in Pennsylvania way back in the late 70s was not unheard of, nor likewise respected and Anne was deemed therein-after as loose, a floozy, a woman of no principles and no decent man would give her a second glance, apart from Jonah Ray! In fact he would have given his right arm for a single positive glance in his direction, no matter the gossip.

The poor deluded, six foot tall Jonah who had zero sex appeal or chance of ever offering the vivacious Anne anything more than a pot of honey from one of his many productive bee hives, which he did from time to time, despite his muscular and strong physique.

In fact, it was the incident at school with the bee swarm that ignited his initial interest in beekeeping, seeing Anne's alarmed reaction to being stung and his knowing that it was all her own fault. He wanted to impress her by telling her what to administer as a means to neutralise the pain, avoid the swelling and itching afterwards. He felt that by imparting this knowledge he would win some favour and thus gain some form of acceptance.

He hadn't deemed to talk about his endeavour with his mother because he had no doubt of any support or encouragement, not having even the wherewithal or inclination to ask how he was coping with his chores of planting, feeding, ploughing and sowing. She was just biding her time until she succumbed to her demise. She no longer felt uncomfortable with her young son having to tend to her toileting, bathing, feeding. Something a son should never have to see or do. She no longer cared, unlike Jonah who despised the weight of responsibility he was carrying.

He relished the time he could spend alone with his precious bees, learning their behaviour, what caused unrest and aggression, or rather, defensiveness as he knew they were not aggressive by nature.

Apart from his bees, Jonah had another hobby, one that he kept under wraps, his secret hobby that he wanted no one to know about. Photography!

Eva was born on a Tuesday morning at 7.30 am. Tuesday's child is full of grace. Anne rejoiced, reciting the nursery rhyme she'd heard her mother and grandmother recite over every birth in their families, feeling blissfully happy that her first born was born on the sabbath - 'and the child born on the Sabbath day, is bonny and blithe, good and gay'.

She felt blessed, she had two beautiful, healthy children. Her mother, however did not share her joy and was mortally embarrassed every Sunday morning when walking into church with her daughter and illegitimate grandchildren, smiling through gritted teeth as picus heads turned in their direction, forgetting that she was, in fact, only reliving everything her own mother went through.

Sunday church attendances were almost mandatory, with everybody donning their best attire for the occasion. Most of Anne's old school friends were there, those still unmarried and living at home under the usual strict regime of their parents who seemingly were loath to acknowledge or welcome the new era of liberation and independence. The female friends mostly, with many of the boys still in Vietnam, fighting the other 'American War'. The names of the fallen would be read out by the sleazy pastor, feigning sympathy and proclamations of heroism whilst hiding shamefully behind the dressage associated with all that is supposed to represent - the ultimate source of purity, truth, Godliness.

Anne was no naive fool, now. She once believed that the pastor was one of God's representatives and that his word had come from The Almighty, thus doing his requested bidding. As she'd matured, though, reading more of the Bible and understood its scriptures, she knew she had been hoodwinked and that the fake person in the pastoral vestments on the podium was nothing but a coward, one who deserved to be behind bars!

She also knew that she was more of a good Christian than he who was preaching about Christianity and pretending to be one. Oh, how she longed to reveal his true identity, see him sweat and squirm and lie his way out, denying her the opportunity to be absolved until the tide turned and the focus of shame and regret shifted back to its rightful origins. She hadn't been the first, nor was she the last, but she was damned if there were to be more!

How many other siblings did her Trevor and Eva have? She counted heads in the church pews, scrutinising the children, assessing any similarities, always wondering.

Anne smiled her customary smile to Jonah, as she did in recognition to the other familiar faces she passed as they made their way to be seated.

"And now please turn to page 204 in your hymn books, 'O come, all ye faithful'."

Anne couldn't help but smirk, *how ironic!*

10: The Incident

Over twelve months had passed since Trevor had been taken to his solitary cell, down to 'the club', to endure the boredom and monotony of his punishment before his final expiry date. He was approaching his twentieth year.

He had yet to witness 'the song of the executioners' as Cole had once described the procedure, with many of the inmates being detained for years, such as Cole himself.

"But why do they do this to us, torturing us this way, keep us waiting in a perpetual state of total uncertainty for however long they do? Why don't they get it over and done with, put everyone out of their misery? Surely, it's to everyone's advantage that all you murders get your just desert quickly, 'an eye for an eye' kinda thing."

Cole's eyebrows raised at hearing Brown's analogy of the justice system and assumption that everyone in the same boat as he, was a murderer!

"No execution will be carried out until such time they can be adamant, a thousand times positive, none of us condemned is innocent."

"But isn't that why you have a jury? Isn't it their job to prove your guilt or otherwise?"

"Human beings make mistakes, kid. Didn't your own jury make a mistake?" Cole replied sarcastically.

"Yes, but yours didn't. I'm working on my exoneration so I guess I'm lucky in that executions aren't carried out immediately, otherwise they will have killed an innocent man, but when it's obvious that a person is guilty, I say hurry up and get the job done, patronise the tax payers."

"Ah, the voice of such compassion and wisdom. Doubt you'd air such views if your date was set for next week. You'd be banging on the door demanding an appeal, a retrial..."

"Well, of course I would! What do you think I've spent the last twelve months doing here? Saving up to go to the Bahamas for a holiday, enjoying all the culinary delights of this exclusive hotel we're staying in, brushing up on my acting skills to become a Hollywood celebrity? What planet are you on? You might be sitting back there accepting your fate because you know you deserve it, but that doesn't mean I have to. No sir, I have faith and one day you will get to witness me walking out of here a free man again."

"A Hollywood celebrity, hey? You already have your desired notoriety, in case you forgot, but this is no Hollywood movie you're in. Ah, but of course, you're relying on your big superstar payday, your compensation for… for… what was it again kid? Defamation of character?"

"That, and mental anxiety, psychological abuse, wrongful incarceration. I've made a list and sent it to my lawyer."

The conversation ended for a while and 'the club' fell silent. There were four cells in their row, two at the top of the corridor, and two at the end. Both side by side, thus disallowing each prisoner to see each other. Their only contact was through conversation.

Conversation with other 'clubbers' aside, solitary confinement was exactly that. No visitors were ever allowed in the cells, apart from the correction facility administrators, supervisors, sanitary members of staff, cleaners. Meals were brought to the cells and were eaten solitarily.

Exercise and showering took place daily and always supervised, always restrained with handcuffs, chains, leg irons, going to and from the areas of purpose. Cells were searched on a regular basis, sometimes daily - depending on if the inmate was deemed problematic.

One single member of staff was never permitted to enter 'the club', it had to be a minimum of two and at irregular times.

"I need to use the library."

"I thought you went yesterday."

"I did, but I forgot to look up a word in the dictionary. Anyway, so what? I'm allowed to go whenever I want to."

"What word do you wanna know?"

"Psychological."

"That's easy. It means ones' state of mind. You're welcome."

"I know that! I just can't spell it."

"Psycho. Logical. It's simple. You know that film, Psycho. Bates Motel? Then add logical on the end."

"Hey, I remember that film with that weirdo son keeping his dead mother's corpse in the place. Can you imagine the smell? Now if anyone deserved to be on death row it was that Norman chap. What happened to him in the end, I can't remember how he ended up?"

"He was put in front of a firing squad last week, did you not hear? Went out kickin' and screamin' like a big baby, professing his innocence, just like you will." Cole chuckled, unable to resist a moment of satisfaction, poking fun.

"You're a nasty, horrible person, Mr. Caveman, it's no wonder you never have any visitors. It's obvious no one likes you. Is that why Ryder calls you 'Caveman', because you're wild and ugly, uncivilised and violent? Primitive, and likes to manhandle women?"

Trevor had turned the tables of humour back to Cole who would have ordinarily laughed at being the butt of someone else's joke, but the kid had overstepped the mark, pressing buttons that were painfully close to home. He had a split second to consider whether or not to retaliate, knowing that a weakness revealed would be fuel for the future.

"Shut your god-damned mouth you little piece of shit before I break through these bars and shut it permanently. I'll rip your ugly head off your scrawny shoulders and shove that vile tongue of yours so far up your tight little fanny you'll be speaking like an asshole for the rest of your pathetic short life!"

Trevor, though shocked, found the whole fiasco entertaining, amusing, and wanted to add a little more fuel to the fire. The boredom was being lifted and he was determined to prolong it for as long as he possibly could, knowing the administrators would be along too soon to regain calm and order.

"Have I touched a raw nerve, Mr. Caveman, like someone did before? The jealous lover perhaps? Is that it? Did she find you boring and take a better man, a *real* man not a cave dweller who could give her what you couldn't? Hahaha, it is isn't it? You killed him because *he* made her feel like a real woman, something you couldn't do. Oh, have I hurt your feelings 'old chap' like they did, ridiculed your masculinity?"

Cole was on his feet, grabbing his cell doors and shaking them as violently as he could. He was incensed and felt his pulses throbbing, his face distorting with rage, spittle flying out of his clenched jaws. He was screeching obscenities through a yearning and desperation to squeeze the last breath out of the voice from the adjacent cell.

He paced backwards and forwards, upturned his bed, threw his chair against the sink. It was as though he was unleashing a lifetime of anger and he was nowhere near wanting to calm down. It felt therapeutic, it felt good. He punched the walls screaming like a demented tortured animal, his knuckles bleeding as he pounded and pounded on concrete, trying to break through to the other side.

Then all of a sudden, he stopped. The staff had obviously heard the fracas and came storming in, batons raised, handcuffs jingling. He was sweating as he tried to regulate his breathing, closing his eyes as if not to see the tormented vision of the past.

His cell was in the same state of wrack and ruin as his mind and body and he cared not one jot. He had longed for his execution date, to be released from the eternal pain of recurring nightmares. Why had God forsaken him, he asked a billion times. He begged to be free, knowing his freedom of guilt would come at the behest of another, one that wouldn't be condemned for his actions. Why were *his* prayers never answered when it was supposed to be written that every man's sins were? What had he done so wrong as to make the Lord punish him for so many agonising, pointless years? Had all his good deeds been dismissed?

Ryder and Pinkstone opened the cell door, surprised to see the devastation of 5216 - aka 'The Caveman' - as he sat dejectedly on the floor, his blooded hands covering his head, both wondering what had caused the man to falter. He'd been the easiest of prisoners over the years, never rising to the bait, as if in total acceptance of what was meant to be.

Hammond, the one still on leave, actually liked the man, practically daring to secretly admire him for his phlegmatic nature and acceptance of everything he was dealt.

There were some like that on death row. Individuals that made them wonder what possessed them to flip, a momentary lapse of insanity, or not. It wasn't their job to judge but it was human nature to, after all. In their jurisdiction, the guilty should be punished and felt duty bound to dish it out where and whenever possible. Make the bastards suffer any which way. A justifiable means of revenge on behalf of the still-suffering families.

Ryder felt certain he heard a sob escape from his prisoner and felt a slight – albeit momentarily - pang of pity as he assessed the destruction of the cell, knowing it would take days to repair. It was evident he would need medical assistance, his hands badly damaged.

The associate, Pinkstone, knelt down in front of the forlorn Cole, feeling no threat to his well-being. The man looked spent, devoid of any will to carry on being.

"Cave, we gotta take you upstairs, man. Get these hands of yours cleaned up, your room repaired, and I have to cuff you too, man. You know that. Get on your feet and let's take you outta here. You ain't gonna cause us any trouble are you, cos if you do, you know…"

Cole opened his eyes cautiously and looked about his surroundings in astonishment as if remembering nothing. He rose slowly, eyes scanning, wondering. He winced at the pain when Ryder cuffed him roughly, dragging the metal handcuffs across his blooded knuckles, knowing full well the satisfaction he would be getting.

11: The Warden Calls a Meeting

Hammond was seated at the Boardroom glass-topped table, the one just expensively restored after some juvenile delinquent of a lawyer bashed his ridiculously expensive watch down on it. The apparently unbreakable glass had a weak spot and shattered into a million tiny pieces, shocking everyone seated around it. Hammond's letter to request a return to his employment was tucked into his jacket pocket… His convalescence period was coming to an end and he was eager to get back to the job he enjoyed, his self-claimed duty to society.

Grey haired Warden Statham walked in, immaculately attired in a jet-black Armani suit, his diamond studded cuff links sneaking to portray their opulence under his jacket sleeves, his Chanel aftershave lingering in his wake, accompanied by his model-like red-headed PA who was going to take shorthand notes. Ryder and Pinkstone were at her heels like obliging puppy dogs. It was 10.30 a.m. Friday June 13, a jug of water already placed on the table alongside a coffee machine, with all its accoutrements.

"Gentlemen, I've read your reports on Cave, prisoner 5216 and I have to say I am saddened. The medical report shows a couple of nasty knuckle fractures, several superficial wounds. Nothing untoward, but he's going to need surgery on his hands and I'm not a happy bunny! This type of shit does not sit well with me on my patch, especially with the likes of Cave, and I'm holding you all responsible. You are the carers of that section and everything that happens down there is up to you guys."

The warden continued, "Any other inmate in this facility is a foregone conclusion but this one isn't, and I want to know the details. Cave has never given us a reason to doubt his integrity, hence his prolonged reprieve, it's never been fully determined - his guilt, at least not a hundred percent as far as I'm concerned, so you understand the reason for this meeting, to ascertain the whys and wherefores."

"Ryder, this is your regular patch, I've yet to see anything in your reports that leads me to see any change in pattern of behaviour, the usual death-row syndromes conducive to the majority of the condemned, so tell me what triggered this particular display of aggression from 5216, this rarity in particular."

Ryder cleared his throat before speaking, "Sir, the caveman hasn't... Sorry, Cave - hasn't before given any reason to – "

"The Caveman? Is this how you refer to him? Pinkstone, is this the name you deem to address him by, The Caveman?"

"No, sir, never. I believe that is the nickname he's been assigned by his fellow... "

"I want that stopped, now! Nobody is to be referred to any other name than that of his surname or prison number, is that understood? If he needs to be moved to another section, so be it, or move those that call him by that repulsive description. They are still human beings under our care and what little dignity they still have needs to be maintained for their own sanity, or what's left of it."

"Are you gentlemen forgetting that these men have been left here to die, their last days, months or years are in our hands. Their well-being or not is at our disposal and it's up to us to allow them a shred of decency before they depart."

Hammond, Ryder, and Pinkstone remained silent. Warden Statham was a compassionate man, fair, and by no means a fool. He'd never warmed to Hammond, despised Ryder, yet something told him that Pinkstone was in a different category altogether: he displayed an air of empathy and a sense of wrongdoing that the others lacked; which could be construed in differing ways, depending on whose corner he was fighting.

He liked the man, Cave. He considered he was detaching his opinions from the outside perspective and channelling his morals in the here and now, to a fellow human being. Which was no mean feat when dealing with the worst of hardened, barbaric, despicable criminals.

Warden Statham was no stranger to feeling the men under his jurisdiction deserved everything coming to them, for they had forsaken every mortal right to sympathy and kindness. Indeed, that's why there were all here, on death row, to pay for the atrocities they committed, because atrocities they doubtless were!

12: After the Incident

Ryder's agenda hadn't always been the same as Hammond's, in the early days; he started off with the same mindset as Pinkstone - do unto others as you would have them do unto you. Live by the 'Golden Rule', etc. However, he'd seen so much, heard the stories, read things he wasn't supposed to read, and somehow, seemingly overnight, he became judge, jury, and executioner - literally, feeling it almost his given right to inflict suffering to those who'd inflicted worse suffering to the innocents.

He was never going to be big enough, strong enough to dish out physical harm, but mental torture was good enough. Set seeds that would grow into fruition, seeds of torment and ridicule that would fester like a rotting tomato. He would manage to find their Achilles Heel and nurture it, fervently.

His first such conquest had been Bud Rogers, that poor excuse of a man who truly deserved everything coming to him, though then it hadn't felt that way. His own hands had ended the life of another human being for the first time and he'd sworn never to divulge his feelings nor the last words of the man he'd just sent to his maker.

Earl wondered if the Almighty had an allowance of accepting passage for those 'just doing their job', like those during the wars who were simply doing as they were told, at will to obliterate the enemy. The crack-shot snipers, the governors and generals issuing the orders to advance and kill. The Nazis who forced the women, children, weak and disabled into the gas chambers at the concentration camps, the butchers and those who work in abattoirs. Where did the buck stop? Who made the rules and who did the forgiving because somebody must have given the okay somewhere down the years that murdering is acceptable when it was considered necessary.

And yet, if that was the case, every single god-damned meat eater on the planet deserved to be brought to trial because they, too, are condoning the killing of innocent beings. No justice system in place to protect them - the animals, and no court proceedings to persecute the slaughterers! It was an expected daily occurrence on a massive genocide.

Nobody batted an eyelid upon seeing meat for sale in supermarkets; the consumer oblivious or unbothered as to the traumas the animals would have undoubtedly suffered before being dragged away to be processed, wrapped and displayed in fridges.

It was an elimination process, a need to satisfy a desire Killing, that is. Most living things have it, the need to kill; or a desire. Need versus desire, however, can be different. No human being *needs* to kill to eat or survive. We can live on fruit, vegetables, pulses, etc., but the *desire* to kill is a totally different thing altogether and for different reasons, like the need to feed the desire.

Earl was doing what any paid person employed under the same job description would have to do, justifying his well-paid salary. If it wasn't him, Hammond, or Pinkstone, it would be someone else. It was a job, one that had been legal and acknowledged for centuries, same as that of a prostitute.

Naturally, the Warden had been informed of the incident down below involving 5216 and - like Pinkstone - had been surprised, never having before had to punish Cole, the normally 'model' prisoner.

Disruption and tantrums invariably happened, it was par for the course with 'clubbers' who rebelled against being cooped up in a small room with none of the simplest humane luxuries like feeling the sun on his face, food of his choice, exercise, female company!

Cole had only ever been outside his cell for more than a few hours once in all his years in the penitentiary unit and that was being hospitalised when he needed an operation for an ingrowing toenail or a visit to the dentist. Once again, his behaviour had been exemplary.

The Warden wondered what had triggered Cole's unexplained outburst. Was he losing his mind now, as many - understandably - did? Was this the first of what was to come? Both Ryder and Pinkstone were going to have to submit their reports and hand them in to the Warden the next day. In the meantime, he decided to take a trip to the infirmary.

"Hey! You down there, can you hear me?" Trevor shouted, hoping for some gossip from his fellow 'clubbers', feeling frustrated at now having no one to chat with.

"I said, can you hear me?"

Two voices echoed back in acknowledgement, "Yeah, we can hear you. What's up, feeling the need to wind someone else up because if so, forget it, Pal, you're not worth the energy."

Trevor was disgruntled: how dare they assume it was his fault? The man obviously had a screw loose and was losing the plot, flipped because he couldn't handle the stark truth. Well, tough!

"Hey, he started it, man. He disrespected me and I thought us brothers should stick together, back each other up, be friends."

A faint echo of laughter filtered up to Trevor's cell.

"Friends?" came a question back, "the Caveman doesn't need friends like you, none of us does."

"Does anyone know how he is?" Trevor persisted.

Nobody answered.

"I said, does anyone know how he is? How can I find out if he's okay? "

"Perhaps you could write to him, you know, send him one of your begging letters to ask for his forgiveness, make him a 'get well soon' card."

Roars of laughter followed.

"Idiots!" Trevor seethed, "ignorant idiots."

Trevor didn't feel the slightest bit guilty. He'd retaliated to Cole's cruel and hurtful remark which had been unnecessary and thus prompted his need to hurt back. How was he to know how the fool would react to a serving of his own medicine?

Shouting out to the two other inmates had achieved nothing so he decided not to pursue any further futile interaction. He took out his notepad to write a bit more of his book, or perhaps a letter to his sister? No. Not his sister, nor his mother.

'The pastor paid another visit this evening. It was Sunday and we'd just finished supper. Mom was clearing the chicken carcass from the table when we heard the rapping on the front door, Eva was sitting in her highchair, her face and hands covered in mashed potatoes and gravy, and Grandma had fallen asleep at the table, her mouth wide open as her head lolled backwards and forwards. My aunt went to open the door and she let the pastor inside. Mom looked disappointed to see our vicar patting my aunt on her bottom as he followed her inside and I couldn't

understand why, because my aunt was a lovely lady and Mom did the same thing to me and Eva and we would both laugh.

I remember the pastor asking my mother for a dram as he sat at our table but I didn't know what a dram was, wondering if it was perhaps a musical instrument similar to a drum and wondered why would he be asking for a musical instrument, was he going to play us some music? It was then that I learned a dram was a measure of whisky and he asked for three glasses to be poured, all the time smiling as he patted my aunt on her arm, her head, but my mother refused and I was surprised because nobody refused our pastor anything.

I remember the pastor standing in front of my mother, confrontationally, my grandmother belching loudly from her slumber and I laughed out loud. Grandma would be mortified to know that she belched in front of our pastor.

I was confused to see my mother's face frowning when we'd all had a lovely Sunday, and visitors were always welcomed in our home. As was proof when just then, Jonah knocked on our door too, walking straight in because the door was open, and he had a huge jar of delicious honey in his hands and a bag of corn cobs, my favourites!

Unbeknown to me, Jonah had come to take us all for a ride in his truck and that made us all very happy, because surprises were rare in our household. It also felt strange because normally after supper, Mom would bath Eva and me and get us ready for bed.

I remember when I was growing up feeling a little uncomfortable around Jonah. He was this huge black, muscular man with a deep voice, but actually a nice face which went all funny when he spoke to our mom. I always thought him more of an imbecile because he kept himself to himself, working his farm, always sitting alone in church.

Apparently his and my grandmother used to be best friends, but they fell out and my grandmother speaks very derogatorily about Jonah's mom, I don't know why, shouldn't she feel sorry for her old friend, being bedridden and all that? Not having daughters and grandchildren? I think my grandmother needs to read more scriptures in the bible and practise more of what she preaches! Take a leaf out of our pastor's blessed book.'

Trevor read these early writings of his, recalling childhood memories. It felt good to lose himself in the past, the good old days when life was carefree and the only thing he had to worry about was appeasing his mother to do his dreaded homework.

He wondered what they were all doing these days, how she felt about him, did her face still light up when she thought or talked about him, was he still her reason for living? He didn't know. He had never set eyes on his mother or sister since the day he was led away, shackled and shamed.

'Hey Caveman, I think we both owe each other an apology. Get well soon.'

Cole lay on the metal infirmary bed on top of a crisp white, purposely provided, cotton sheet. His bandaged hands resting on his stomach above his pyjama bottoms, his closed eyes enjoying the warmth of the sun's rays through the heavily-barred windows, and considered every broken bone and suture well worth the pain to experience a different environment, the ministrations of a non-judgemental doctor. It was akin to being on holiday. He had been somewhat unaware of Warden Statham sitting aside his bed, disturbing his dreamlike state, until he heard voices.

"He can return now, Warden. There's no reason for him to stay here any longer. His bones will heal over the next few weeks, but he'll need assistance with toileting and showering, possibly eating too, at least for a day or two until he manages by himself. Why? His condition isn't life-threatening, he just won't be able to play the piano again."

The Warden dismissed his last comment as glibly as it was delivered. "When was the last time he had a psychiatric assessment?" he asked, studying his surroundings, scrutinising various framed medical certificates hanging on the walls.

"You do realise that if Cave is diagnosed as mentally ill, with - what? Schizophrenia, bi-polar disorder, depression, something else, his stay of execution could be prolonged. This, erm, unusual display of self-destruction is not normal behaviour for this particular prisoner, wouldn't you agree?"

The doctor seemed to read between the Warden's lines, knowing that 5216 had never been a problematic case, "I can arrange an assessment…"

Cole jumped up from his bed, "You'll do no such frickin' thing. You both know damned well there's nothing mentally wrong with me. The kid just touched a raw nerve, that's all it was. Look, I'm stitched up and ready to get back to my hotel room, stop fannying about and get me back on track. I'm sorry for all the unnecessary trouble I've caused, truly. Feel free to dock the restoration work money from this month's salary for my hotel room and let's all get back to normal."

Cole continued, "Warden, the kindest thing you can do for me is to persuade the governor to hurry along the proceedings, get the damn show on the road."

But the Warden wasn't easily convinced or placated.

"Are you daring to question my integrity, Mr. Cave? Please don't flatter yourself that the State's correctional facility grant any olive branches or indeed favours to you boys. You don't *get* to request kindness, or has that slipped your mind? I will decide whether or not you will be returned to your previous abode, me alone, not the doctor here, not you… me! How many years have we known each other, Cave?"

"With respect, sir, we *don't* know each other."

"And yet we are of similar same age, are we not? Walked the same paths, learned the same things at school and no doubt both had the same ambitions, all those years ago. Would it be reasonable of me to assume we both revered the same sports personalities and yearned to emulate them? McEnroe was mine, 'you cannot be serious' hahaha. What a player! I wanted to be him, a professional tennis player. I was good, too. How about you, Cave, who was your hero?"

Cole reflected momentarily, trying to think back to relate to the Warden's memories, questioning his own dreams and ambitions, and remembering his own private tennis lessons. Did Statham know that, too?

"No one, sir. I didn't have anyone to hero worship, no role model to look up to - apart from Christ of course - guess you could say I was your average loser."

"An 'average loser'? Hmm. By choice or destiny?"

Cole was becoming irritated by the Warden's drawn out trial of analysing everything.

"You tell me, sir, there are plenty of experts receiving mega bucks to tell you exactly what you need to know about me, but I am not, and I don't care. Are we done here? Because I'm tired. All this talking has exhausted me."

"Don't you write your songs any more, Cole?"

Cole frowned. He knew the Warden would know every single detail about him, and inwardly cursed him for bringing up the subject.

"Or rather I should reiterate: 'Why don't you write your songs any more, Cole?'. You let others claim fame and notoriety through your works and…"

Cole cut him off. "And now I have a different notoriety? Either way they're only words. Words are just a mixture of letters, you know. In every language you can think of; it boils down to mere scribblings, not dissimilar to the hieroglyphics found in and on ancient monuments. The reader will decipher and interpret whatever they want, it doesn't matter. Nothing really does, does it? We're born, we die. That's it. I'm done."

The Warden nodded his understanding, "That may be so, but I'm not, and it's my prerogative to pull rank and so I'll continue with what I was going to say. I'm considering allowing you a week's respite, to recuperate, heal. Extend the hospitality a fraction."

Cole had already sat back on the bed, listening to the Warden, watching the doctor writing notes, seemingly feigning interest in the conversation.

"Begging your pardon, Warden, I'd just like to go home now, there's nothing like the comfort of one's own bed, the familiar luxuries we indulge ourselves in, the friendly chit-chat of ones' neighbours. I'm sure this good doctor here has more pressing things to occupy his time than molly-coddle a worthless piece of shit like me. Can't you sign my release papers and take me back to the club house?"

"Not now, no. The doctor has informed me that you will need help with certain functions and so you will have an auxiliary come to assist you until such time as you're able to manage by yourself. Besides, your 'home' isn't ready yet, the sanitary ware is being replaced and replacements don't arrive until after the weekend. Take advantage of this situation for a while, Cave, consider yourself on a lucky break. Tell me, what can I get for you?"

"I suppose a rope or a razor blade are out of the question?" Cole replied blankly.

The Warden sighed heavily as he sat back down on the chair, his hands knitted together on his lap. He suddenly felt embarrassed at his evidence of normality, his fine clothes, jewellery, coiffure, acknowledging how it must appear to the pitiful man lying before him, who wasn't allowed even the luxury of a wet shave, a daily ablution performed by millions without a second thought.

"Your humour isn't lost on me, Cave, but I am human." He paused, thinking of something significant to add.

"If you can think of something *realistic,* I'll see what I can arrange… for the duration of your hospitalisation, you understand. While you *are* here, you are a patient and your treatment will be as that."

Cole knew that the Warden was trying to placate him. He was a decent enough sort anyway, and with his hands broken and bandaged he felt certain that they all assumed he could do no harm to either himself or anything. His manacled ankles would ensure he wouldn't be going far either!

"Oh, before I leave, there's just one more thing, not that I doubt you, may I say, but you will have 24 hour surveillance. State rules and all that, I'm sure you expected nothing less, so you won't have total freedom. I'll pop back tomorrow to see how you're progressing."

Warden Statham walked briskly back to his office. He wanted to pull out the files on 5216, find out more about him. There were a couple of men in his facility that didn't seem to fit with the conceived notion of a dangerous criminal yet he had no reason to question the decisions made in courts by experienced lawyers, judges, those who'd undergone long trials, unscrupulous testimonies proving beyond a shadow of doubt as to the authenticity for their incarceration and verdict.

In Statham's opinion, Cave had accepted his fate far too easily, never putting up much of a defence, agreeing too readily to the prosecutors' barrage of accusations. But was he wasting his valuable time, trying to find a loophole somewhere that could exonerate him when for the past decade or more, nobody had done?

He also asked himself, 'did it matter?' when clearly public opinion - as well as Cave's own - was bring it on. Put out the bunting and celebrate killing the beast.

Elizabeth, his red-headed PA, was on the telephone when he walked into his office.

"I want you to go down to the archives and arrange to bring up all the files on 5216, have them taken to my car, plus everything in the filing cabinets. I've written out the request forms, fax them over to the governor and send him an email to this effect."

"I'm assuming you mean the digital files, and not the unthinkable amount of boxes. And am I to mention the incident and that he's now in the infirmary?"

Statham considered her question. "He most likely won't have a clue who 5216 is, nor will he be bothered. He'll probably attribute this unfortunate incident to mismanagement and we'll have to undergo a massive disciplinary hearing and retraining of our personnel. I don't know, Elizabeth, what do you think we should do? Oh, and yes, yes of course I didn't mean the boxes, doubt the old jalopy could accommodate them."

Elizabeth was always pleased to hear her boss ask her opinion, it made for a good, professional, working relationship.

"We send a daily report every morning to the Governor's Office so I don't think there's a need to explain anything further, John. When he receives the faxed request he might raise his thick white eyebrows and ask why, but until then, I can't see any need to perpetuate his stomach ulcer. Looking for anything in particular?"

Statham laughed out loud, picturing in his mind the grossly overweight governor, sitting at his dining table with a large Cuban cigar and a tumbler of whisky, surrounded by patronising associates revelling in his equally overweight wife's outlandish yet feeble attempt at hospitality, when all she had to do was pass over the duty to a paid member of staff, then dress for the occasion.

John Statham and his wife of thirty years, Isabel, had endured a couple of such lavish and excruciating events over the years and had loathed them. It was always the same thing with the same pompous pricks every time, levitating their status above those in their care; those 'lower deck' waiting to be eliminated from society.

"I honestly don't know, Elizabeth."

*   *   *   *   *

Doc. Doc… can you turn the light back on please?"

"The light is on, Cave, I haven't turned it off. It's only 5:00 p.m.

Cole squinted, disbelievingly. It didn't seem as if the room was illuminated. It felt dark and cold. He shivered.

The doctor walked over to his bed and noticed Cole's body shaking, a sure sign of the ague.

"Your body has gone into shock slightly, it's natural. I'll give you something to stop the shakes. How about a painkiller for your hands?"

Cole's sudden awareness of his unfamiliar surroundings compacted with his ague and when he heard only half of the word 'painkiller' and saw the doctor holding a full syringe of sedatives, he panicked, imagining himself in a horror movie of being immobilised at the hands of a sadistic psychopath, and he yelled his lungs out, and did not stop.

He couldn't move from his hospital bed as his legs were tethered. He was weak, and his hands bandaged. He couldn't even pick his nose or teeth. Inhumanity couldn't stoop much lower if they prevented him from being able to wipe his own ass! Which, of course, he couldn't!

In a moment of absolute self-pity, he whispered 'my God; my God! why hast Thou forsaken me?', leaving the doctor to cringe with embarrassment and wonder if the Warden was indeed correct in his question as to Cole's psychiatric state-of-mind.

It was never a surprise when many 'clubbers' declared finding salvation in Christ after 'seeing the error of their ways' and had repented. They read their Bibles like it was an instruction manual, a hypnotic book on 'how to prove to the universe you're a changed person and belong back in society'.

The doctor knew it wasn't in his job description to make analyses of anyone passing through the infirmary doors, that was under the jurisdiction of the psychoanalysts etc., but it was human nature to wonder where the hell they got their notions of redemption from! Desperation, no doubt. And who could blame them?

"It's a sedative to stop the ague, that's all. It will help you to rest and forget your pain for tonight. I'll leave the light on all night if that's what you want."

Cole didn't answer, and by the time the doctor had counted to five, he was already fast asleep.

14: Fourteen Years Earlier

"Another coffee please, Carolyn."

"It's *Caroline,* not *Carolyn* as I've told you umpteen times now, same as she's Janette, not Janet. A trait for you men, I believe, to forget a woman's name. What is that famous quote 'a rose by any other name would smell as sweet?' Not to the owner of the name, we ladies like it pronounced correctly. And yes, thank you, I will have one myself, I'll add a latte to the kitty."

"So, it's *Caroline?* and you say 'a rose by any other name would smell as sweet'? So… I will steal 'Sweet Caroline' from the Diamond himself, but don't tell him. It's Shakespeare by the way, from Romeo and Juliet. You see, I'm a lyricist, I kinda feel a different song coming on. I don't believe I offered you a drink, but OK, I'm good for it."

Caroline was chuckling to herself. She loved tormenting the customers over the pronunciation of her and her colleague's name, most of them invariably getting them mixed up, and confusing them further if they did get it right by telling them the opposite! The repartee made the working hours more enjoyable.

She wanted to continue the banter as she refilled his coffee cup, "I actually tried reading Shakespeare once but found it difficult, excruciating in fact. All that 'where for art thou' was beyond me. Don't misunderstand me, I love the classics, but I prefer to view it from my TV screen. Does that make me a heathen?"

Cole hadn't missed a single thing, aware of the '*I* prefer to watch it', no mention of '*we*'.

Caroline was eighteen years old, short peroxide-bleached hair she wore in a pixie style, which accentuated her big blue eyes and button nose. Cute and childlike was how Cole thought of her. She had an endearing laugh which she bestowed on all her male clients at the diner, mornings, lunchtimes, and afternoons.

It was a stopgap, she'd convinced herself, working at the diner. Earn a tidy amount to get her campervan fixed up, and she would be off in search of her destiny, wherever that may be, until such time she might decide to go back to college.

She had been practising to be a midwife, thoroughly enjoying the training helping to deliver babies, watching them take their first breaths as they emerged into a brand new world. She would watch from a distance as lachrymose parents fascinated over the tiny human-being they'd created, all the time wondering if this was what was expected of her, to become a mother, have a family she could call her very own. There was plenty of time.

"A heathen, for not being able to understand Shakespeare? No, no, no, not at all."

Cole wanted to add that only by dismissing the Holy Scriptures would he categorise her as a heathen but talking religion with a waitress during his lunch break was neither the appropriate time nor the place. He couldn't afford to be late back to work either, so he paid for his food, coffees, left a reasonable tip, and hurried away.

He often felt apprehensive, talking to females, a little awkward deliberating on what to divulge as memories, or how much. Did they even care, the majority? Was his background of relevance, importance? Most people only saw the surface, the facade that was portrayed, nobody had ever got close enough to try to understand him, to look behind the mask. And that suited him perfectly. Thank you very much.

Friday night, October 22, in the mid-1990s, Caroline had driven her campervan to the diner in readiness for her early Monday morning shift, satisfied in the knowledge of her vehicle being roadworthy with the new tyres, replaced cam belt, oil change, etc. Her mode of transport was also her home, accommodating all her worldly goods. It was her sanctuary, and the diner's outside lights offered her the security and safety she needed. She was going to stay one or maybe two more weeks then off to who knew where.

The diner's doors opened precisely at 8:00 a.m. Janette had already gotten several pots of coffee percolating, the condiments on the tables, the pancake mix prepared, eggs and hash browns at the side of the stove, waiting for the influx of customers, watching the clock's hands move closer to 8.15 a.m. and chomping at the bit at the tardiness of her colleague, wondering what was keeping her when she knew she was awake because even though the lights were off, she heard the music coming from her radio.

She was dying for a cigarette and stepped outside to smoke one before switching on the fryers, banging loudly on Caroline's campervan door as she lit up.

"Hurry up, you, come on; I've done all the prep, get yer ass into gear and give me a hand."

She finished her cigarette and stubbed it out with her shoe, disgruntled at receiving no reply from her work colleague.

A car pulled up, a typical family truck type. Janette hated these customers, the ones who left such a mess, helped themselves to all the packets of sugar and sauces, and never ever left a decent tip! Privileged and spoilt fat kids who demanded everything, then threw temper tantrums when being told there was no ice cream! The customers that Caroline dealt with and flattered the parents as to how beautiful and well behaved their little darlings were, how they resembled their parents, etc., was a trick Janette had never been able to muster. She loathed children.

But this wasn't the normal family carload, this was a family of diverse race. The mother a stunning black beauty, her partner slightly lighter skinned yet a huge brute, and their two children could have been easily have been mistaken for Caucasian, incredibly well behaved, too.

"Trevor, would you like some pancakes for breakfast, with blueberries or maple syrup?" Anne asked.

Trevor looked to the waitress who was standing by the table pouring coffees, "do you have scrambled eggs and hash browns?"

"Sure do, but it will take a few minutes, the best hash browns in all of Pennsylvania can't be done in a matter of seconds. You prepared to wait?"

Trevor nodded, smiling expectantly, deciding this was indeed worth waiting for. He'd only ever had hash browns once in his nine years.

Janette was now seething; she had to cope with the family's order plus the other regulars now coming in, wanting their regulars, and Caroline still hadn't condescended to make an appearance, and it was now 9.00 a.m., an hour late!

She refilled the coffee cups for the family then nonchalantly excused herself, saying she was going to rouse her work colleague from her campervan, declaring jovially that the idle-good-for-nothing needed to be whipped into getting her act together.

Janette's fury was increasing. She'd spent the last hour getting everything ready to start the day's trading, administering to those already patronising the establishment, smiling a fake smile whilst begrudgingly conjuring something resembling edible to those seated.

She banged harder on the campervan door, this time omitting any niceties because she was pissed off, big time!

"It smells."

Janette looked to her side where the voice came from and saw the young boy who'd asked for hash browns, standing next to her. She turned to him, surprised to see him there.

"What smells?"

The boy pointed to the door of Caroline's home. "There," he said, "it smells like poo."

Janette hadn't noticed at first, but after the boy pointed it out, she, too, detected an unpleasant odour. She hammered more aggressively on the door.

"Caroline. Caroline! Open the frickin' door, for crying out loud! I know you're awake! We can hear the radio and we've got a shedload of customers screaming for their breakfast. You're not being fair, now open the door and give me a hand."

Nothing, but the sound of the radio.

"I found a dead dog once, at the church. It was in the well. It stunk; I think a dead dog is in there."

It certainly couldn't have been Caroline's toilet that caused that awful gagging smell. It was the kind that the boy described upon finding a dead animal, that sickening putrid, unforgettable smell of decay, and Janette began to feel panicky.

She was enveloped, temporarily, in a situation of bewilderment. It was totally unbelievable that the boy was correct and that her work colleague could be dead, decaying, inches from their view. There was bound to be the surprise element of her appearance and some pathetic excuse as to her lateness.

"It *must* be her toilet. She probably hasn't managed to empty it because her campervan has had to have a lot of works done on it. It's one of those chemical things that has to be emptied every now and again. We're lucky that we don't have to do that, aren't we? We just go and flush."

"I don't," Trevor stated, proudly, "I don't like to waste all that water. I just pee outside. Do you know how many gallons of water it takes to flush? It's a waste of natural resources. If we didn't get any rain we wouldn't have any water and then we couldn't survive. Same as bees, we couldn't survive without them, either. Jonah keeps bees, lots of them. He makes honey from them, too. Did you know that honey was found in the pyramids and was still edible? Imagine that, no sell-by dates!"

Janette looked at the boy who was trying to educate her in subjects she had no desire to know of, and then looked back at the door of her friend's campervan, beginning to go beyond annoyed.

"911, what's your emergency?"

"It's my work colleague, my friend, she's not answering her door and I've been knocking for over an hour," said a frantic Janette.

"And it smells of dead dog, tell them that, too," piped up the little know-all who was jumping up trying to look through the windows.

"… and there's a very unpleasant odour coming from her vehicle."

15: Matt Hansome, Attorney at Law

Matt called for Elaine, his PA, to bring him a cup of coffee while he read through his morning's mail, he was gasping and it was only just after 9:00 a.m.

Monday mornings always started with the same reluctance of tearing himself away from his beautiful wife in the warmth of their bed, from feeling agitated at the amount of traffic on the road as he navigated the journey to his office, to the very thought of ploughing through another week of red tape and bureaucracy, all the time wishing for Friday afternoon to come round again.

It was the same old, same old. Counting his blessings on one hand because his profession afforded them a very comfortable lifestyle, and cursing it on the other wishing he'd taken a different career path, one that didn't involve trying to defend the guilty, like a car mechanic, a landscape gardener, or even a professional sportsman.

He loved soccer, wanted to be – and was good enough to be - professional but his father insisted he go to college, get a degree and a 'proper' job, declaring sports people have only a limited time to earn the big bucks.

Elaine placed a cafetière on his desk and his usual mug. No milk, no sugar, just the way he liked it.

"Another begging letter from our Mr. Brown I see, Matt. Do you want me to write him the same reply?"

Matt sighed, the man was very persistent. Always the same content, always proclaiming injustice and his need to be pardoned. Matt doubted there was a guilty person on death row, they were ALL innocent if you were to believe them! He couldn't be bothered to actually read it, knowing what it was going to say yet again.

"I'm far too busy to keep doing this, month after month. I honestly don't understand where his train of thought is. He knows I can't do anything, his sentence was a foregone conclusion, the guy's not an idiot. In fact, his IQ was amazingly high, considering. No, leave it, Elaine, I'll at least give him the courtesy of reading it. It's just that unfortunately I don't have as much time to waste as he does."

"Well, actually, Matt, he doesn't have 'time to waste', does he? He's never going to become an old man, is he? Can't blame any of them for trying for a second chance, and he was adamant he was innocent from day one."

Matt remembered everything about Trevor Brown and his declarations of innocence, but he didn't need his PA's advice or her two cents' worth. She hadn't been the one whose parents splashed out a fortune on sending him to college and law school, eventually graduating after years. She was just a glorified secretary, shorthand typist, coffee maker!

"Well, after I've read his letter, I'll let you reply in your usual aplomb of diplomacy and sympathies, I'm sure you'll find the right words to give him a modicum of hope and encouragement that the State is doing everything it can to accommodate his request, seeing as though you have nothing better to do."

"Oh dear, Matt, sorry if I've jumped in where I shouldn't, I certainly didn't mean to belittle the court's judgement, it's just that I think…

Matt's eyebrows raised to listen to her continue.

"Well, he really does believe he's been wrongly incarcerated and that's why he keeps writing to you, perhaps I can find some words of encouragement to send him, like you say. Surely, they all benefit from having something to hope for?"

"'All', you say? All of them on death row should be allowed to have something to hope for, like their victims, would you say? When you type up the court notes, statements, see the photographs of mutilated bodies in the files wouldn't you agree that those would have 'hoped' to have been spared their lives? Their grieving families would have most certainly 'hoped' that their loved ones were still alive, and not begging for mercy like they would undoubtedly have been.

I'm sure if it was your daughter, son, mother, whatever, being brought to the forensics in body bags, lying dismembered in the cemetery due to the insane actions of a demented rapist, knife-man, you would not care a jot if they 'hoped' for a single darned thing ever again! They gave up the right of any decent human being's care the minute they made their sick choice. 'Thou shalt not kill', remember?"

"Yes, and isn't another one 'Thou shall not commit adultery'? I'd better fetch you another coffee, Matthew, your mouth's wide open, must be dry!" Her stinging sarcastic tone made Matt squirm in his seat.

It was one time only, and in a moment of alcohol-fuelled madness which he regretted deeply once he'd sobered up and realised his gross stupidity. He was dreading returning to work the following Monday morning knowing he was going to have to face his PA and hoping (!) that she wouldn't take it as a beginning of anything. He loved his wife and was petrified of his dirty secret coming to light. Naturally their little tete-a-tete had boosted Elaine's confidence where her job was concerned, giving her an invincibility that she could do nor say anything wrong. Times he felt like he was walking on egg shells, this very conversation being typically so.

Matt knew he should eat humble pie if he was going to keep her sweet. Her silence was imperative, as well as maintaining a harmonious working relationship.

"I apologise, Elaine. I was rude to you and you're right, everyone does have an opinion. Just because my opinion differs from yours doesn't absolve me from speaking to any member of staff like that. Look, here's twenty dollars, go and buy us all a couple of donuts. "

She snatched the proffered twenty-dollar bill, smirking victoriously, grabbed her handbag and headed for the door. She'd keep the change!

16: Jonah

Twenty hives took a lot of time and effort to maintain, but beekeeping was a hobby he thoroughly enjoyed. It was something out of the norm and he'd garnered a lot of respect from his neighbours, notwithstanding that already gleaned due to the commitment he made regarding administering to his aged bedridden mother.

Nobody pointed the finger at Jonah for his failure to join the throngs to go to fight in Vietnam, back then, totally understanding his predicament. He could not leave the farm, nor his disabled mother, much as he'd desired to. Everybody needed to eat and a strong man like Jonah was much in demand on neighbouring farms.

He had harboured feelings of guilt for years over this, recalling his childhood pals who had gone to do their duty and never returned home, their names remembered in Sunday services by the creepy pastor who Jonah couldn't stand. He wouldn't reveal to anyone exactly *why* he didn't like him, it was a gut feeling, at first, he always swore by first impressions.

And church was church, mandatory attendance to Jonah's way of thinking, to offer thanks to the Lord for his lonely existence and silently pray to be released from his burdens.

He'd had no life to speak of; no adoring father or role models to revere. No siblings to play with and not a single person he could class as a true friend, and it perturbed him; never understanding why. There was nothing abnormal about him, he wasn't stupid, and he never saw himself as ugly, in fact he dared to consider himself a cut above his peers due to his stature and strength.

He used to dream of becoming a basketball player, a baseball player, a soccer player but speed wasn't on his side, neither was good fortune. He was more of a lumberer, a bumbler, ploughing his way through his school days.

It was the bees that made him something of an enigma in his town and it captivated his every thought. The school incident had provided an avenue to dissociate himself from everything, negative, to a degree. He wanted to learn as much as possible about beekeeping, how to produce honey, how to recognise situations that would provoke attacks, how to build hives and cultivate colonies.

He desperately wanted to impress Anne Brown, too, to show her that he was worthy of her attention. Though he struggled to get there over the years, he finally succeeded the day he went to deliver a pot of honey and a sack of corn cobs, having heard the pastor's motorcar pull up outside Anne's house.

The look of relief on Anne's face as he let himself in was all he needed to see. The look of defeat on the pastor's face was gloriously satisfying, knowing that the next Sunday's sermon was bound to be on the lines of 'thou shalt love thy neighbour as thyself' which would make his hackles rise. Jonah knew what the creep was about, he had the photos, a whole box full!

"Jonah, what made you decide to start breeding bees?" asked Trevor, standing with outstretched arms towards the dripping honeycomb Jonah was offering him.

Jonah looked up to the skies as if trying to recall the exact minutiae, then back at the young boy, "Your mother!"

"My mother! But she's scared of bees, ever since she got stung by one."

Jonah laughed out loud, "She did, and so did others in our class but it was a sight to behold I tell you, Trevor. Can you imagine a classroom filled with bees, it was like a dark cloud hovering above us. The kids were scared cos they'd never seen anything like it before, and when you've never seen the likes before, it does make you worry."

"I wouldn't have been scared. I'm not scared of anything."

"Then that makes you a very brave and strong young man, Trevor."

"You're not scared of anything, either. You're already strong, you can do anything," he answered back.

Jonah smiled, thinking 'oh to see ourselves as others see us'. "As we grow older, we fear different things. Uncertainties can be scary, things out of our control. Life is uncertain and scary."

"No it's not!" Trevor replied indignantly. "How can life be scary? It's exciting because there's so much to see and learn and that's why I watch the television a lot because it's much better than school. Our brains are like sponges, you know, they absorb everything. We have five senses: smell, taste, sound, touch, sight. Some people are really lucky and have six cos they see ghosts and stuff, but not all humans have that sixth sense. Do you?"

Jonah grinned, "I don't, no. And I'm glad I don't because as I say, that would be scary wouldn't it, to see ghosts, things we don't understand?"

"Why would seeing a ghost be scary? I'd love to see one, I would have so many questions to ask it, wouldn't you? I'd talk to it and ask it what it felt like to die and what's it like in Heaven. Is Heaven just another planet in the galaxy and is God the owner of the Heaven? Does He make all the decisions as to who goes there rather than Hell? I'd ask the ghost if all the animals go to Heaven, even those we've eaten because it's not their fault is it and it's not our fault that we've eaten them? I think it must be very crowded in Heaven with everybody that's died, those in the wars, the tsunamis, all the animals, and insects, do you think there is more life in Heaven than what's here on Earth? Could there be more dead things up there than what's living here, now?"

Jonah was somewhat agog and didn't know how to respond, the boy had obviously been giving it a lot of thought.

"I don't wanna ask the pastor because I don't think he really knows, I think he only pretends to know all the answers, like a fake pastor."

"What makes you think that, Trevor?" Jonah had his own opinion of the sly pastor, and it wasn't a favourable one. He was keen to hear the youngster continue with his explanation.

Trevor huffed, "In my grandma's Bible I read that Jesus said 'suffer the little children unto me' but when the pastor comes to our house, he doesn't practice what he preaches and tells my mom to send me and Eva to bed so he can talk with her and my aunt but I can tell that Mom doesn't want to. I wish I was grown up and strong, like you, so that I could protect my family; sometimes I want to kill him."

Everybody knew that Trevor had a wild and vivid imagination and a passion for airing his views on everything. He was the type of child his grandmother declared 'had been here before', certainly one that would never go unnoticed, or unheard.

"Trevor, boy, what in Jesus' name makes you say such a thing? You wanna kill the pastor, the man who represents God? The man who preaches the way of the Lord, teaches us all about how to be a better man and love thy neighbour as thyself?"

"Jonah! Duh! You forgot to add 'he who is without sin cast the first stone', and 'do unto others as you would wish to be done by'. I know what the rules are, all the commandments, but I think the pastor has forgotten or decided to make some new ones because I know he steals things and that's not right is it? A pastor should not steal, should he?"

"Unfortunately not everybody lives by the same rules, there are those who say rules are made to be broken, and absolve themselves by going to church every Sunday, begging forgiveness and consider the deed done, but then they have to live with their own conscience, if they even have one. What makes you say the pastor steals things? That's a big accusation."

"If I tell you, that makes me a snitch, doesn't it?" Trevor searched Jonah's face for some type of confirmation or reassurance to continue to offload the knowledge he was dying to impart to someone willing to listen to him.

"It depends. You have to ask yourself if it's important for someone else to know what it is that you think you know. What is the purpose of sharing such knowledge and is it going to be detrimental to the person who wants to keep whatever it is a secret. I can't help you make your decision, Trevor. Only you can do that."

Trevor thought long and hard.

"Your bees keep secrets, don't they? They fly all over the place and I bet they see things we will never see because they're really small and can get into tiny crevices. They can't tell anyone what they know, same as animals and birds, and ghosts. But the Holy Ghost can talk can't it? it must be able to because the pastor talks to it."

Jonah was totally out of his depth, not knowing how to deal with the inquisitive mind of the boy.

"What's virginity?" he asked, staring beseechingly at the big man.

Jonah gulped. He hadn't considered a question of that nature!

"Well," he stuttered, "that is a lady's most precious virtue. You know of the Virgin Mary, the mother of Jesus? Her virginity has been held in high esteem for centuries because she kept hers and yet she was able to produce the son of God. It's something like a miracle really."

Trevor considered his answer. "So if someone stole someone's virginity does that make them a saint or a sinner, because stealing *is* a sin, right?"

Jonah jumped up in disbelief, he couldn't handle any more bizarre questions to which he had no answers.

"Boy, where do you come up with these notions? You're asking the wrong person, I don't have a clue. Why don't you ask the damn pastor? He's the one who will supposedly have all your answers."

Trevor jumped up too, "Don't you understand why I can't ask him? Because he's the thief! I heard my mom tell my aunt that he stole hers and he was trying to steal my aunt's, too. Why would the pastor want to steal from my family? That's why I want to kill him because we're not rich. He shouldn't steal; that's one of those ten rules, and he's a fake pastor."

Jonah was gobsmacked. He felt numb after hearing the words from the youngster. Of course, it all now seemed so obvious to him. He'd had his suspicions for years, hence he'd taken a catalogue of photographs, but he didn't realise the depths of depravity their pastor had already reached. Young Trevor Brown wasn't the only one wanting to kill him!

17: Matt Hansome

"Another two letters from Trevor Brown, Matt. One of them requesting you pay him a visit. I feel I'm exhausting all my 'Dear John' replies and I'm actually feeling a bit sorry for him." Elaine placed all his correspondence in front of her boss.

"Save your sympathies for the victims, Elaine. I've told you before. The way he ended that poor sod's life was horrendous, barbaric in fact. What a dreadful and agonising way to die. Spare me your emotions and forget him. He's not worth patronising. What's next?"

Elaine felt she was being dismissed yet she wasn't finished.

"He was just eighteen years old. You said yourself he was incredibly bright with a high IQ, ambitions to become an astronaut so not your average dumbo. He achieved -- "

"He achieved his place behind bars which was justly administered, and don't for one minute think that intellectual people, ultra intelligent people, don't deserve to be punished for their deplorable actions.

"

God, some of the world's notorious killers are exceptionally brilliant manipulators. They're astute, cunning and off the radar a lot of times, that's *why* it takes so long to catch them."

Matt continued, "It wasn't 'a spur of the moment decision' you know, for the jury to reach their decision. I don't have to remind you how many months and thousands of dollars it cost to conclude the man's fate. What? You're saying everybody got it wrong and you know different? You and a handful of others have become expert in law?"

"I'm not saying that. No, I couldn't, but at least I acknowledge that I've become a little more 'expert' in compassion, and I'm so glad I didn't have to sit the same examinations as you as to 'how to become a complete asshole!'"

*　*　*　*　*

Elaine had a high school friend, Trudi, who had always been a magnet for the waifs and strays and underdogs of the world. She had set up a soup kitchen for the homeless, handing out blankets, sanitary products to the females, animal feed to those with dogs because no matter how little they had, they would never forsake their beloved pets even if it meant going without food for themselves.

Elaine remembered vividly her friend's compassion for the persecuted during their school days, she stood steadfast in front of bullies and befriended the friendless. She had an enviable, formidable character that took no rubbish because she didn't need to; Trudi had inherited a fortune after her unspeakably wealthy parents were killed in an air disaster years ago. She was fourteen years old and point blank refused to go into care, declaring that her best friend's mother had agreed to give her a home until she was of age to go back to her family home, which bewildered Elaine's mother as she had no recollection of offering any such thing.

Trudi was very much her own person, mature beyond her years. Even though Child Protective Services acquiesced, allowing her to live with Elaine's family, she barely spent a night there, only popping back to attend the obligatory social services visits. And she was a good girl; arranging all her finances with the bank manager, ensuring everything was always covered. Her parents had taught her well.

She had no intention of ever getting on a plane and flying off to exotic locations, feeling that her inherited wealth would benefit a lot of people less fortunate. She eventually dropped out of school, feeling it unnecessary to learn a trade she had no interest in pursuing, she only wanted to help those in dire need.

Over the years she had seen off dozens of potential gold-diggers who tried their charms on her but failed miserably. She wasn't interested in high school heartthrobs or celebrities' sons and she didn't need anyone to look after her because she could look after herself. She *liked* doing the 'looking after'. It made her feel useful, worthwhile, and so she eventually set up the soup kitchen to help the ones who weren't lucky enough to be in the financial position she was in. She, too, could have been out there on the streets, begging for handouts, there but for the grace of God.

She did it all in style too, spending her inheritance wisely. She hired a couple who had been living on the streets for years, gave them back a chance to reclaim their dignity, a purpose to look after their own, and she also wanted to learn about those incarcerated, those who weren't afforded the simplicity of enjoying food in the company of friends under a starlit night or able to luxuriate in a shower without the dread of reprisals from inmates.

Prison intrigued Trudi. She wondered how they coped being cooped up, especially those on death row, the ones she'd watched on TV and those she'd read about, some having no one at all pay a visit. Many of their families had disowned them for their crimes and she wondered what magnitude of evil would make a mother forgo her love for her child or a wife that vowed to love and cherish her partner for better, for worse.

She had a yearning to know what depravation was deemed acceptable enough to wipe away those loyalties, vows, and love. How could anyone simply switch off, dismiss, like flicking off an irritating flickering light bulb?

"Trudi, I think I might have found someone you'd like to talk to. You know, you said you always wanted to have a bash at befriending someone on death row."

Trudi had just lit a cigarette and had taken a sip of her glass of red wine. It was Friday night and the two friends invariably got together once a month to catch up, enjoy the craic and a bottle or two.

"Are you talking about that young chap, the one that Matt's adamant deserves everything coming to him but you're not so sure?"

"No, of course, I'm sure. Yes, it is the young chap, but just because I'm suggesting him doesn't mean that I'm suggesting he's not guilty. Oh, flippin' heck, you know what I mean. I just kinda feel a tad of pity for the guy, that's all, and you've said a hundred times that you'd like the opportunity to get inside their heads."

"I didn't exactly say that I'd like to get inside their heads because I would imagine all the shrinks have already tried that angle and their expertise is unquestionable. What *I* wanted to do was to offer an olive branch of friendship, someone to reach out to, become something like a pen-pal. He's obviously got under your skin. Why don't you do it? you've already been writing to him backwards and forwards. You already have a rapport, a better insight, already knowing everything about him."

"I couldn't possibly do that! It's totally against all rules, and besides, Matt would most definitely fire me! I'm too close to his case, Trudi, that's why I'm suggesting you write to him."

Trudi smiled, "You could always pretend to be someone else, write to him under a pseudonym."

Elaine, too, was smiling at her friend's suggestion as she poured them both a refill, "I could. I could pretend to be you, but this is your opportunity. Why are you reluctant?"

"Because, come on, Elaine, I've met some sorry and sad excuses for people over the years but I've not willingly or knowingly had a one-to-one conversation with a murderer! Perhaps I need a little time to consider it first and evaluate my commitments before you race ahead and put the wheels in motion. I've no intention of becoming one of those delusional saddos that think they're going to fall in love with a death rower and work tirelessly to redeem them."

Elaine laughed out loud, "Trevor's barely twenty-years-old Trudi. You're almost old enough to be his mother. In fact his mother *is* about our age if I recall. Never been to visit him as far as I can remember, nor his sister. We're notified of visitations, naturally, as Matt has to know everything about his clients." She tried to think back to the case notes she'd typed up wondering what his sister's name was; damned if she could remember. Emma? Eva? Something on the lines going through her brain channels of memory was thinking Eve, as in the Garden of Eden, tempting Adam with the Apple. The guilty innocent, or the innocence of the guilty.

18: Six Months Later: Cole, Back in 'The Club'

Seven days after Cole's 'respite' in the infirmary, he was taken back to his pitiful but instantly recognisable surroundings, despite the newly installed sanitary ware and decorated walls. It was like *deja vu* when he sat on his familiar grey blanket and hardly a minute had passed when he heard that familiar irritating sound of the reason for his hospitalisation, "Hey, Cole, welcome home."

'Welcome' was a seven-lettered word that felt anything but, and 'home' was an obscure dimension in relation to his surroundings and predicament.

The very words 'Welcome Home' were meant as a warm greeting, to be joyous about a happy reunion. A huge banner above the threshold surrounded by familiar smiley faces and party poppers exploding alongside corks from champagne bottles. If only…

Cole could hardly muster a reply. He'd enjoyed the solitude of his own company, different types of conversations with the doctor and warden, when necessary, but his little reprieve was over now and it was back to the normal waiting game.

Cole and Trevor had never actually *seen* each other. All cells on death row prevented any kind of visual friendship, but they all formed visions in their mind what they thought the others looked like, inventing their persona.

Trevor imagined Cole was black, like himself; tall, strong, and muscular like Jonah, perhaps even with a broken nose and multiple scars from fighting. He wondered if he had ever done any boxing.

But Cole was nothing as Trevor pictured. He was white, for one thing, practically bald now, average height and average looks, but he had a beautiful deep, almost hypnotic voice. He was soft-spoken, usually, and would always speak words of wisdom, quoting parables or reciting certain anecdotes when conversing with Trevor.

Cole *might* have pictured his neighbour as a tall, lanky pathetic white boy with long greasy hair and soft hands, never having done a hard day's work in his life. The typical rich college kid whose besotted parents indulged his every whim. No doubt he would have had an expensive car gifted to him on his sixteenth birthday as many did these days. He would have undoubtedly seen the world and travelled to expensive and exotic locations that Cole could only dream about. He might have conjured up this image, but he didn't.

And yet, Cole told himself, they were equals at this stage. No amount of money was going to buy their freedom, no amount of anything was, only a whacking miracle of which they'd prayed futilely for. They were the same, here. Every single one of them.

The days blurred into months and even though Cole had decided he was bound for the flames of Hell, he considered it a better alternative to his current existence. Whoever decided to make a man wait years for the execution of their sentence was indeed a criminal in his own right. It was inhumane. Hang us, inject us, electrocute or shoot us, for God's sake! Just put us out of our misery.

"I received a letter from a woman," Trevor stated. "Like a pen-pal letter, really."

"That's nice, I suppose?" Cole answered unenthusiastically.

"It is!" He replied, "it's exciting to receive mail from the outside, I don't get anything from my family... I wonder why she decided to write to me and not you, or any of the others. Has anyone ever written to you?"

"No." Cole's tone was meant to put an end to the conversation, but as usual, the boy missed it.

"What about your lady friend? Or your family? You never talk about your family; do you have any?"

Cole was reluctant to take the bait, but sometimes it actually felt good to have someone show a little interest; it broke the boredom of silence. Nevertheless, he sighed, "We all have family; some good, some bad, most dysfunctional, and some invisible."

"Invisible? What? you mean like dead family, ghosts?"

"Yeah, something like that. 'Skeletons in closets' kinda thing. Kids we might have and not know about, you know. You got any kids, boy?"

"Me! No, of course not, I've never even been married."

"That don't surprise me, considering what an ugly bastard you are," he whispered.

"What did you say?"

"I said 'that surprises me, considering what a clever bastard you are', what's wrong with the women in your college?" He'd raised his voice to make himself heard.

"Oh, I wasn't in college, only high school. After my grandmother died and we paid for the burial, my mother struggled financially. It took everything to keep a roof over our heads and now... Well, I don't know, Cole. I don't know how she's managing to survive without me and I feel so guilty because now that he's... and I'm... and she doesn't write or visit but that's probably because she's struggling to finance the trip here, do you think?"

"People will always find a way to pay for what they want.'

"How did you do that yourself?"

"What? Oh. A bit of this and a lot of the other. Took anything that paid enough dollars to eat and enjoy myself. A grumbling belly has no conscience. A man has to do what he can to survive the big wide world."

"As long as 'the man' abides by the rules and doesn't hurt anyone whilst he's trying to survive, you forgot to add. No one should be burdened with a guilty conscience for the rest of their lives, that would be too painful, like a self-inflicted type of torture. A festering wound unable to heal."

"Ah, of course, I'm forgetting that I'm talking to the one and only innocent here in 'the club', please forgive the selfish ramblings of an evil entity… and… Shut the fuck up!"

"Her name's Trudi, and I can read you her letter, if you want to hear."

"Don't make me lose my temper again, kid. Ha, on second thoughts do me a favour and send me back to the infirmary."

"Just listen… I'll only read a little bit. *'Dear Trevor, I've finally plucked up the courage to send you a few short lines in the hope that you'd be willing to correspond with me. It's the first time I've done anything like this so I'm not even sure if you will receive this, but here goes, in anticipation.'* And then she's put a laughing face."

"What the hell is a laughing face?" Cole's time in prison began before emojis came into vogue.

"It's a picture of a laughing face with tears coming out of the eyes, there are many different kinds of emojis you can use. She's typed the letter, you see."

"I see!" He didn't see.

'I know what it feels like to be alone, scared, abandoned. Nobody to hear your thoughts or worries, or even your hopes. I was fourteen years old when my life shattered into a million pieces and hadn't a clue how to climb out of the abyss, but - as it was a case of sink or swim - I decided on the latter; I had no alternative.'"

"My heart's bleeding," Cole said sarcastically. "How much more do I have to suffer?"

"You don't actually, I don't wanna share any more with you. She's written to me and I'm going to write back to her like she asked."

Cole was suddenly disgruntled, surprised to realise that he *did* want to hear more, but Trevor would not budge.

"So, she send a picture with her letter?" asked Cole in his attempt to glean more about the writer of the letter.

"No." Trevor was playing him back at his own game.

"She say where she from?"

"No."

"Then how in God's name you gonna reply to her if she didn't send you her address?"

"Goodnight, Cole. Don't let the bed bugs bite."

Cole was furious. The boy was taking advantage of his vulnerability. The lights went out almost mockingly, reminding them of the long and dark hours until the morning. The hours that would be flooded with thoughts and regrets, memories and dreams. He knew that Trevor was eloquent; like himself, they both liked words and he was secretly a little envious that his neighbour now had someone interested enough to correspond.

Cole thought back to the warden's question, '*why don't you write lyrics anymore?*' Well, what's the point? He asked himself. Who would be interested to read the words of a lifer? Carolyn had been interested in reading his lyrics - or was that Caroline?

19: Anne

Anne had been incredibly thankful for Jonah's intervention that Sunday afternoon, walking in laden with corn and honey, all those years ago. She called it his 'divine intervention' because since that very day no one saw hide nor hair of the pastor ever again. He simply disappeared, leaving the Sunday church congregation turning around in the pews, muttering quietly, at a loss as to when or if the pastor was going to make his usual appearance.

Half an hour passed before Jonah decided to take the rostrum, gazing across the sea of expectant faces staring up at him.

"If the pianist is ready, can we all sing the second verse only of hymn number 19, To be a Pilgrim?" The pianist played a brief introduction of the melody known as *"St. Dunstans"* before the congregation joined in.

"Who so beset him round with dismal stories,

do but themselves confound, his strength the more is.

No foes shall stay his might, though he with giants fight;"

As the verse ended, they all stared at Jonah waiting for him to enlighten them as to the meaning of his choice of hymn.

He felt somewhat out of his depth with all eyes and ears on him, trying hard not to focus just on the beautiful face of Anne who stood proud with her children at her side, clearly understanding his reasoning and feeling an overwhelming sense of gratitude. She viewed him in a totally new light that Sunday morning, realising that love sometimes was blind, it was simply a case of having the blinkers removed.

And that was how Jonah and his school crush became a couple. And what a delightful and handsome couple they made, too. Nobody questioned the parentage of Anne's children because Jonah was also light skinned and nobody had any reason to think that Anne and Jonah were half siblings because the rivalry between their two mothers had been kept under wraps for their entire lives.

After Jonah's mother passed, he found and read her diaries and was finally able to understand his father's animosity. It was all there, in his mother's own handwriting, how she'd only ever loved one man, Carlton Brown. Carlton Brown, senior! She was very descriptive and revealing in her diaries, and Jonah had felt guilty reading her private thoughts, initially; but then it became an obsession, a need to know. It also devastated him to wonder if – in fact - Anne could be his half-sister.

It was obvious that Anne's father and Jonah's mother had been in love, and his mother had written of a passionate, consummate love, nothing close to how he viewed his two parents. He wondered what had happened all those years ago to make his mother forsake her marital vows?

One passage in his mother's diaries haunted his sleep one night, and he couldn't make sense of it. She wrote, 'when love encompasses everything one is taught as sacred, how is one supposed to exist without it? I cannot, nor do I want to live another second without feeling the glorious intimacy of my love.' He knew who she was referring to.

Jonah stacked away his mother's private scribblings. It was his legacy from his mother and he felt he should honour her secret and never breathe a word to anyone.

His farm work and especially his bees afforded him a different allegiance, a more… what was that feeling? A more responsible, parental almost, dimension. They depended on him and he them; he was delighted when young Trevor took an interest, pestering Jonah constantly to pass on his knowledge, so much so that his mother's 'friend' decided to get him a hive of his own. The youngster was no fool and learned quickly, revelling in the attention he was getting, and hell bent on being as proficient in beekeeping as his mentor. He couldn't wait until he was able to taste his very own honey.

Trevor's conversation revolved entirely around beekeeping. He knew he had to respect them and tread softly because Jonah had warned him over and over of the consequences of an angry hive. In all his years of keeping bees, Jonah had never suffered a single sting! His hives were incredibly healthy and productive and was a godsend to all the local farmers.

Eva was approaching her birthday. She was going to be five and was not looking forward to starting school. She didn't want to make friends, as her mother constantly told her she would, once she had settled in at school. Her mother insisted that she would learn lots of new things, new skills, a whole new world would open to her but Eva still sulked about the prospect daily.

"I understand you, Eva," her brother told her, "I think it's a waste of time, too. The television learns you a lot better than the teachers."

Anne interrupted, "And that just goes to prove my point that school is essential for you both, young man, because your command of the English language is abysmal! A television cannot *learn* you anything; it's *teaches.* You *learn* from being taught. A teacher teaches, and a learner learns."

Trevor and Eva regarded their mother, "Why is it not *teached* then? If the teacher teached me something why does it have to be *taught*?"

Anne felt smug. "Why don't you ask your teacher when you go back to school after the holiday, I'm sure she'll *learn* you!"

"But you just said it was… "

"Exactly! Go to school and learn how to speak correctly. Get educated before you're too old. Oh, I get that you think you know it all already, but believe me sunshine, you know nothing. Astronauts have to be highly educated people. NASA can't have any idiot in charge of a spacecraft zooming up into the atmosphere can they?"

"I'm not an idiot, Mom," he answered dejectedly, hurt at his mother's words.

"Trevor, I'm your mother! I *know* you're no idiot, you are an exceptionally bright boy and I have no doubt that you are gonna make me one proud mama one day. In fact, you've already achieved that, but just imagine how far you will go when you've got years of learning under your belt. You too, Eva. People never stop learning because nobody could ever know every single thing there is to know. Anyway, get ready, both of you, Jonah's coming over in a few minutes to take us all out for the day. We're going to stop off at the diner for breakfast and then drive into town to pick out a special birthday treat for Eva.

That was the day Trevor experienced his second viewing of a dead dog. When the police received no reply to knocking on Caroline's campervan door, they tried the handle and lo-and-behold the door opened effortlessly, the putrid stench forcing them to take steps backwards, covering their noses in disgust, and Janette retching violently.

The police officer immediately shut the door and called for an ambulance, assuming what or whoever was decaying inside would be beyond the help of any medical assistance, but the ever-inquisitive Trevor was determined to prove himself, dismissing the overpowering smell of decay and stood stock still, jaw open, in a moment of *deja vu* when he saw the corpse of a once beautiful young golden retriever nailed to the ceiling of Caroline's pristine campervan, its tongue hanging from its mouth, its legs cruelly dangling unsupported, her once soft brown eyes filmed unseeingly.

"I told you," he exclaimed over and over, "I told you it was a dead dog. Who would want to kill a dog as beautiful as this golden retriever? They're not bad dogs."

Everyone looked at each other in confusion. If it was just a dead dog inside, where was the young woman's colleague? And who did the dog belong to?

Janette spoke first. "A golden retriever? There's only one person I know who has that breed of dog, a regular of ours, Foxy. He comes here practically every day, he and Gwinnie, Guinevere. She's as good as gold, that girl. Who on God's earth could think of doing something bad to her? Foxy adores his dog, and so does Caroline! Oh crikey, I'm gonna be sick again."

Anne, Jonah, and Eva, had now left the diner to join the outside activity, wondering what was keeping everyone and why there was such an influx of vehicles with flashing lights.

"Mom!" cried Trevor, "it's another dead dog, I told them it was. I remembered the smell from before; remember when I found that one in the old well by the church?"

Dogs went missing on a regular basis in their small town in Pennsylvania: the affluent buying expensive pure-bred puppies who lost their 'cute' appeal once the designer shoes and furnishings had been chewed beyond salvageable, their puppy behaviour too much trouble to put in an effort to curtail. Of course, the over-excused 'gone to a farm with more open space', or 'someone with more experience and time on their hands to better care for them' became the normal term of phrase to describe the animal's absence.

Trevor's first encounter with a deceased dog never left him. The smell, however, had been difficult to remember whereas the visual memory was as unforgettable as seeing a first shooting star zooming across the sky in a moment so unexpected: the shock, the thrill, the excitement, not so different yet on a totally obscure dimension. Usually memories didn't come with smells; they're tucked away somewhere in the memory bank. It's the visual memories that are easier to recall, like looking back on a photograph. Sounds and smells almost non-existent unless something triggers those senses, like a song or a perfume which can transport one back to who knows where.

Anne remembered that dreadful day her son had come running in to tell her he had found something awful in the old well at the church. It was a hot sunny Friday evening, late August. They'd been to the churchyard to lay some flowers on a relative's grave and young Trevor had been asked to draw some water from the well. He'd struggled to wind up the bucket, puffing and panting at each action of the task. The smell hit him before the sight of the mutilated animal, its eyes open wide in shock, its tongue lolling from its mouth. As the water dripped from the bucket, Trevor stared at the unfortunate creature, saddened to see such despair on an innocent being in sacred grounds, remembering the priest's sermons of a proverb in the New Testament, '*I desire mercy and not sacrifice*'. He wondered who had made the sacrifice he witnessed and what mercy had been withheld.

Jonah put one of his huge conforming hands on Trevor's shoulders, "I think we should go and leave these experts to do their work. There's nothing we can do here: let's not make this a sad birthday for Eva to remember.

"It's okay, I don't mind. Can I go inside and have a look?" Eva asked.

Both Anne and Jonah exclaimed simultaneously, "No!", at the same time as Trevor had declared a profound "Yes!" They were spared any further discussions as the police officer stood in front of the campervan door, barring anyone from entering.

Jonah paid the bill for their breakfast and hurried everyone back inside his truck, keen to get away from the unfortunate encounter and eager to continue their day trip.

"It's not fair," Eva whispered to her brother as she sat beside him in the back seat, "you saw the dead dog. Why wouldn't they let *me*?"

20: Caroline and Foxy

Caroline had been shocked to see a police vehicle and a distraught Janette outside her campervan when she pulled up with Foxy outside the diner, wondering what all the commotion was about, already having rehearsed her apology for being late.

Janette glimpsed her friend's arrival. Alighting from Foxy's vehicle, Caroline's expression mirrored Janette's look of shock/disbelief/relief; the myriad of emotions circumventing her thought process.

"Janette, sorry, I'm SO sorry for being late, Gwinnie went missing on Friday night and we've spent the whole weekend looking for her. We still haven't been able to locate her and you know what Gwinnie is like. She never leaves Foxy's side. He's beside himself with worry. I'm sorry I'm late but what are those policemen doing in my campervan? What's happened here?"

Caroline was striding towards her home but Janette stopped her. "Don't go there… please… it's Gwinnie."

"Oh, she's here! How on earth did she get here? Why didn't you call me and let me know? We've been worried sick. Foxy hasn't been able to focus on anything since she disappeared and we've looked everywhere for her. We never dreamt she'd come here. The poor girl must be starving *and* traumatised. Is she OK? Oh, thank goodness you found her, Janette, he's going to be so relieved, you can't imagine . . ."

Janette stood facing her friend, putting her hands on her shoulders, "Caroline. Gwinnie is inside your campervan, but please don't let Foxy inside to see her, and it's best you don't, either."

"Oh stop the dramatics, Janette, just let Foxy collect her and I'll get my ass into gear to make up the time I've lost this morning. What? An hour or two? Nobody died so it's not gonna be too much of a hardship at the end of the day, is it?"

Caroline stopped in mid-sentence, cocked her head to the side, and wrinkled her nose. "What *is* that awful smell?

Foxy was heartbroken, inconsolable in fact. He couldn't imagine who would want to hurt his beautiful dog and why she'd been so cruelly 'displayed' in Caroline's campervan. How had she even got there? Everybody at the diner knew Gwinnie and she was never an ounce of trouble, just happy to lie underneath the tables, ever ready to accept a pancake treat or a friendly pat on the head.

Cole would hear the elongated saga later that afternoon when he'd finished work. He sat listening to Caroline's tears, no longer eager to hear more of the lyrics he'd been keen to show her, the ones he'd been brimming with excitement over and rushed back on Friday evening to wait for her to finish so he could anticipate her reaction. He'd been surprised to see her walk out of the diner with Foxy and his dog, laughing together like a knowing, young courting couple. He sat in his vehicle while they went inside her campervan, then five minutes later they drove off together in the old pick-up.

Cole found himself getting angrier and angrier, and realised he was intensely jealous. Why would she want a long-haired, tattooed, bohemian waste-of-space like Foxy when she could have a more mature, more cultured man like himself? His jealously manifested into a feeling of having been ridiculed and strung along. He decided they needed to be taught a lesson they wouldn't forget.

First, he needed to hit back at Foxy and give him a large dose of pain. Let him suffer that feeling of loss and dejection like he was feeling. He would then decide how to repay Caroline because she, too, deserved to be punished for her wanton behaviour.

The dog had been an easy kill. They always were; especially the domesticated animals, so trusting and gullible once a piece of meat was dangled before them. People, though, they were different. No chance of a strapping young man being lured away by a measly bit of old sausage on a string there. No sir! It took planning, cunning, strength, tactics, patience, and intelligence. Cole had an abundance of the lot!

"Hey, I'm sorry to be a party-pooper today, Cole, but I can't stop thinking about poor Guinevere and Foxy. Who would do something like that, I ask you? And why did they put her in my home? Neither of us thought about coming back here to look for her. Do you think one of the regular customers could be responsible?"

"Who knows the mysteries of life? Perhaps she hurt someone and they wanted revenge?"

"Gwinnie, hurt anyone? Revenge? Absolutely no way, that dog wouldn't hurt a fly. No…" She pondered, slowly, "that looked like a message, as if the person responsible was leaving a note, and I don't know who it was for. Me or Foxy."

"Can I show you the lyrics I've written, I spent all last week.. "

"Sorry, Cole, I'm really not in the mood. My mind's on overdrive and I can't even go back into the van now until I've had it cleaned. I'm staying with Foxy for a few days until it's done. More coffee?"

No, he didn't want more coffee. She'd just put the final nail in the coffin!

*　*　*　*　*

Foxy's decomposed head would be found six months later by a group of teenage boys fishing for crayfish in a small creek twenty miles from the diner. His other body parts took weeks longer to surface. Caroline had been the last person to see him. Her hair was found in his bed, lipstick on a wine glass. His dog had been found dead in her campervan. It was well known that she was planning on a road trip and was trying to accumulate the funds to do it. There was money missing from Foxy's apartment along with a priceless Gibson guitar he'd inherited from his grandfather.

Cole had been long gone; bored with the dramatics of Caroline, bored with the tedium of waiting for something new to arouse him. His tolerance level for the mundane was waning. He needed new stimulation, young blood, forbidden fruit, the ultimate climax.

*   *   *   *

Is evil born, or the result of life, upbringing? Many experts would declare a baby is born pure, and that is indisputable, but even the well-bred, the loved and adored can harbour a ghoulish agenda, given certain mitigating circumstances. A reason to be heard, seen, understood, or not. Envy, for example: that old adage, relating back to Biblical times of Joseph and his brothers. How they envied him and the love their father bestowed upon their younger brother. The very same envy Cole Perkins felt towards his own baby sibling.

Cole Perkins had spent his formative years of his life surrounded by adoration and love. His seventeen-year-old mother and thirty-eight-year-old father saturated him with an abundance of opulence and attention. He wanted for nothing, materialistically or otherwise. The undivided attention of wealthy parentage provided him an envious education. He grew to be eloquent, cultured, clever. He was spoilt beyond imagination.

His crooked teeth were corrected. He had his own private tennis coach twice a week. His father took him to every basketball game the Roosters played, come rain or shine. It was only when his brother arrived on the scene twelve years later that he felt a shift in his thoughts, something he'd never experienced before.

With his mother nearing thirty and his father approaching his fiftieth year, he now had a rival sibling, and it troubled him because he didn't know how to handle this festering resentment. His father stopped taking him to the games because he was hell bent on splashing out on extravagant parties, inviting friends and acquaintances over to welcome his new heir, wanting to show off their new baby.

Cole was feeling more and more redundant, neglected, no longer their centre of attention. Why was he no longer enough? He cringed watching his mother breastfeed his new brother, seething with envy as both parents overlooked him. He hated seeing their smiley faces and covered his ears at their laughter at the simplest of gurgles or smiles the baby would perform.

It was all just far too much.

*   *   *   *

Cole's mother was Rosetta Cave: his father, William Elijah Perkins. Their first born was christened Cole Elijah Perkins; the new baby, Alan Issac Perkins. Cole eventually decided to change his surname from Perkins to Cave – his mother's maiden name. He liked his biblical middle name and therefore would keep that. He would never be known as Cole Elijah Perkins ever again.

He left his home that night in the wake of his own destruction, his annihilation. He felt no remorse, just a feeling of euphoria and liberation to pursue his destiny. His rucksack was bulging with dollars and jewellery he'd taken from his father's safe. He cared not an iota as he mounted his motorcycle, the flames to his family mansion burning violently behind him.

21: Warden Statham

Statham had spent weeks going through the files of 5216. He'd forgotten that Cave had been previously named Cole Elijah Perkins, until it stared him in the face.

It had been a waste of time after all, he decided, now attributing Cole's lack of participation on the stand as pure nonchalance to his horrific crimes. He wondered if the man realised his depravity and that's why he was so steadfast to have his sentence administered. Most in 'the club' constantly professed their innocence and strove towards getting a new hearing, anything to stall the inevitable, yearning for redemption. But not Cave.

He really was a sick individual, Statham admitted. There was no end to his brutality and various crimes. Animals, men, women, children, often using a different alias depending on location and the employment he undertook.

With a heavy heart, Statham switched off his PC and removed the discs. He'd read enough, enough to discontinue any further sympathies.

"You sick, sick bastard!" He muttered to himself. "Your own family; innocent people who never did you a wrong turn. Trying to pretend you're an honourable man when you're worse than dog shit. Enough now, enough. I'm gonna make your dream a reality, 'Caveman'; it's time."

*   *   *   *   *

"Hey! I got a reply from that Trudi," Trevor exclaimed.

"How romantic," scoffed Cole as he sat on his bed concentrating on picking his toenails.

"There's a slight smell of something on the paper." Trevor sniffed deeply to inhale the scent.

"It will be the disinfectant. The bosses have to disinfect their hands before handling mail. They have to wipe each piece of paper with an impregnated cloth to remove any possible trace of drugs. That's why we're not allowed to receive books from the outside."

"Really? I didn't know that. But that doesn't apply to writing materials, I guess?" Cole didn't reply.

"Yeah, it does, actually. I can smell chemicals. Actually, you know what? It's kinda nice having a pen-pal; I'm going to conjure up an image of her, like those guys did in that film 'Weird Science'. Do you remember? They fed all their ideas into a computer and made their ideal woman. She was beautiful. I bet Trudi looks just like her, stunning. She'll have long dark hair and big brown eyes. Painted fingernails and matching toenails. I bet she's real smart, too."

"She can't be *that* smart if she's written to you."

Trevor ignored the sarcasm, "Trudi Hopkins. Perhaps she'll want to meet up with me when I get out. She could be waiting outside with all the press surrounding her, cheering me on waving her arms above her head and screaming my name…"

"Oh, spare me any more, please! She's just an attention seeker like so many others of her ilk. She's not interested in you. She's just gonna love telling all her pals that she's writing to a 'clubber' purely for the sympathy vote. I bet she'll read out your replies to all those who give a shit and they'll be having a good old laugh about you. Hah! I can hear *Ms Hopkins* now, '*gather round everyone, while I read his latest tales of crap'.* I thought you were supposed to be intelligent!"

"Oh, I think you're just jealous cos she chose me, and you've never had a woman choose you. Is that it, hey? A touch o'the green eyed monster?"

"I did all my own choosing, thank you very much. I chose, I took. That's what God put the weaker sex on this earth for, for man! It's obvious, isn't it? Didn't you ever read that quote 'a woman without her man is nothing'? It's in their make-up to be dominated."

Trevor contemplated his statement for a moment. "My mother was a stickler for proper grammar and pronunciation. She was always learning me, sorry - teaching me the differences between was and were, she and me as opposed to she and I, that kind of stuff, and I think if you reconsider that quote and put in commas, it should come across as 'a woman (comma) without her (comma) man is nothing. Two commas alter the whole concept of your quote, making it turn the tables in favour of a woman who is the stronger of the sexes. Not physically, I give you that because generally we men are physically stronger: but emotionally don't you think women have the edge?

They give birth, remember, and I can't see many guys wanting to swap places on that score."

"'A woman, without her, man is nothing'? what a load of rubbish! You change the woman and man around to make the same statement, a damned sight more realistic too! God, you're more of a fool than I gave you credit for. I was right the first time. Women were created for man's pleasure, read the Bible! Eve was created to bring pleasure to Adam, and it worked for a time but, as usual, women don't listen; always thinking they know better. She was warned not to eat the forbidden fruit, but - typical female - refused to adhere to the rules. The rest is history. Amen."

Trevor scoffed. "Well, wouldn't you? If someone told you not to do something because it was wrong, wouldn't you want to try it? And before you answer back immediately, think about your current circumstances. You're not here because you've been the model law abiding citizen, are you?"

Oh, he was good! He knew how far to stick the knife into the raw wound! Cole could almost like Brown – if he didn't despise him so much.

He chose not to reply, refusing to play the cat-and-mouse game with his 'cellie', (not *entirely* a 'cellie', though, because no one shared the same cell in the club). The thing with having such conversations invariably evoked memories, ones which would often invade dreams. The moment the lights went out and all was dark, it was almost impossible not to reminisce about everything. Sometimes it would be thoughts of better, nicer times; others, like watching a movie, re-enacted by a different version of oneself. A hypothetical illusion of seeing a crime committed by an altruistic, detached version of oneself. Sometimes, most times, especially in Cole's case, it was orgasmic.

Foxy's Gibson guitar felt good in his hands. He'd strum to the lyrics he'd written all hours he could to make a decent sound. He knew the popular dulcet tunes that had everyone singing and dancing along to. He could perform the same just as well as those earning the big bucks, if he'd dared to forfeit his past and rise like a Phoenix to a whole new world. Too many 'if only' scenarios. There was no point dwelling on the road behind, that route had already been walked and chalked. Onwards and upwards, new mountains to climb, new thrills to spill, new sins waiting to commit.

Trudi was enjoying the back and forth correspondence with Trevor and found herself looking forward to receiving his replies. He wrote a lot of his personal thoughts without being despondent or full of self-pity. He even managed to include an abundance of humour which would have her throwing her head back in laughter. She asked herself, '*how could anyone in his circumstances find something to joke about?*'

He'd told her how he would like to write a book and had begun to produce a few pages already. She'd lie on her couch with a glass of wine as she read and reread his letters wondering what awful crime this eloquent young man had committed to warrant his current situation. She had asked Elaine if it was possible to read some of his case notes, but Elaine valued her job too much to dare sneak anything out from under Matt's beady eyes, suggesting the better alternative was probably Google.

She wrote about the charity work she was undertaking. He told her he admired this and that she must be a very kind and selfless person. She told him she had lost both her parents and felt utterly lost until she decided to stop feeling sorry for herself and do something useful with her life. He wrote about his own feelings of helplessness, being unable to take care of his mother and his sister.

She had put off her Google search on Trevor Carlton Brown, for now. She wanted to get to know him as he portrayed himself in his letters.

"She's an orphan. Her parents were killed in a plane crash."

"Who's an orphan?" Cole asked, feigning interest.

"Trudi! She helps feed the homeless."

"Ah! The beautiful Ms. Hopkins. That's not a bad thing. At least she doesn't have two demanding, overpowering parents breathing down her neck reminding her what a huge disappointment she is to them. She's lucky, I'd say."

"Yes, I suppose *you* would. I could imagine that your parents would be disappointed in you."

Cole snorted a sinister chuckle, "And you are one paragon of virtue, aren't you? Your mother's pride and joy. I bet she tells everyone how proud she is having a son who's on death row, waiting for his vaccination."

"Won't happen. You'll see. I shouldn't be here, unlike you! You know, Caveman, you should tell me your story because one day I *will* get my story published and it's only fair that I give you a little credence besides what the public have already read about. Why don't you consider it? Let me tell your story too?"

Cole remained silent, thinking of what he'd just heard his delinquent thorn-in-the-side say. Did he really want the world to know about him? His dastardly deeds, his sick acts?

"The Song of the Executioners." Trevor continued, waiting for a reply.

"Hmm. Cool choice of title. You need to acknowledge me for that! But you're wasting your time, kid, you'll be an old man before you finish it, or forever remain a young man if you don't!"

"Whatever. I could just create you as a wretched character here and invent my own stories about you. Some coward I used to talk to, to relieve the boredom everyday. You'd be 'Caveman the Coward' who had 'little man syndrome' and wanted to prove to the world how 'big' he was by carrying out brutal atrocities on unsuspecting females because his masculinity wasn't meeting the desired criteria. A pathetic skinny worthless excuse of a man who could never get it up and satisfy a real woman. Did you ever satisfy a real woman, Cole? Were you able?"

Cole could easily have taken the bait, but controlled his anger by forcing a hearty guffaw.

"Who gives a shit about 'satisfying a woman'? Like I said before, God put them on the earth for us, man! It's their purpose in life to satisfy us. You, virgin boy, wouldn't know anything about it, would you? You would only know how to satisfy yourself and that makes you a total wanker!"

"I believe all men are, in that crude classification of yours, but I don't share your view that women are just there to be taken. Remember, Jesus didn't disrespect women! Take Mary Magdalen, for example. In fact some historians proclaim he married her and they – "

"She was a damned hooker, for crying out loud! Even back in those days, women knew their place, see what I m saying? Women of today need to follow her example more. Bathe their men's feet, give their bodies freely in order to please. It's their duty and destiny to provide sex, reproduce, and cook. They've been allowed far too much freedom over the centuries and that's why the world is in the sorry state it is. Good grief, kid, you really *do* need to read the Bible more to get a better understanding of mankind. You hear that? 'MANkind', not 'womankind'. Hu-*man*, not hu-*woman*. 'God created man in *his* own image', HIS, not HER. It's all there in black and white, all according to the Gospel. Mary Magdalene was a proper woman!"

"Wow! I wonder how you'll be greeted up there, you know, when you're knockin' on Heaven's door? Your Judgement Day, and they say to you 'sorry pal, only the good guys get to pass Go, you gotta go back to jail'? Will you start blubbering like a baby and beg forgiveness?"

"Hah," he scoffed, "don't try to preach to a preacher, I'm ready to meet my maker, have been for a long time.

Looking forward to being introduced to my seventy-two virgins in paradise, too.”

Trevor couldn’t contain his squeals of laughter. He laughed and laughed until his sides hurt.

*   *   *   *   *

“*Dear Trudi,*

Thank you again for your lovely letter, I look forward to them all, eagerly waiting to receive your words. The mood of my day is now determined by you alone. Oh well, that’s not entirely true, sometimes my ‘cellie’ can manage to diffuse my euphoria with his doom and gloom. I think he does it on purpose when I’m feeling optimistic or happy. Actually ‘happy’ isn’t an emotion I feel on a day-to-day basis unless I receive one of your letters, but he’s the king of negativity and is only happy himself when he’s trying to reduce me to his level.

I doubt none of us here would be able to envision a light at the end of the tunnel because we’re all living on borrowed time, as the screws remind us often, but it’s difficult to think about, the ultimate departure from the world. I suppose your parents had the same fears in those moments before they met their fate but at least it must be comforting to you to know it was probably instantaneous and not painfully prolonged, unlike many.

It's a pity you didn't have a sibling with whom you could share your grief, someone who would totally empathise with you, like a younger sister. I have a younger sister, Eva. But there again, no, scrap that thought, my sister is a bad example of sisterly love, which I've learned since being incarcerated. Do you know, she's never once written to me or been to visit? That has saddened me no end because I always considered we had a tight bond. I was that big protective brother for her and I loved her. I still do love her and worry about how she and my mother are coping without me. Perhaps they are still ashamed?

I'm certain my mother believes in me still, I mean I'm sure she believes in my innocence because nobody knows or loves you like your mother, right? She once recited, 'oh the tangled webs we weave when first we venture to deceive' and isn't that profound? It's a beautiful saying but she didn't enlighten me any further because I found it strange she said that and never explained its meaning or purpose.

She can't come to visit me. Can't or won't, I'm not sure which, but I do understand her difficulties. It must be hard for her now, and I can't say I blame her, it's not a place to visit. I wish I had a magic wand to make everything better. I wish my cell was a time machine and I could flick a switch to transport me to another dimension in time. What do you reckon, Trudi? Should I go back or forward? What would you do if you had that opportunity? Would you go back and make that trip with your parents, or talk them out of it altogether?

Tough decision, hey? Cos if you'd gone with your parents and suffered the same demise, then the people you're now helping would have missed out on your hospitality, BUT… you'd be in heaven with your folks, and don't you think that everything is meant to be? Our lives already preordained? I do! Did you know that the twelve signs of the zodiac are supposed to represent our existences on this earth? We're all supposed to be 'here' twelve times, according to the understanding of astrologers, so if your star sign is Pisces, the twelfth sign, you're on your last leg of the astrological cycle, you won't get to be reborn. You're stuffed, basically.

It's fascinating isn't it; the stars and the universe? Think about the word 'infinity'. That alone is enough to blow one's mind, isn't it?

I often think about how it would be to sit in front of you and actually 'talk'. I think we would chat away for hours and hours over an ice cream or coffee, maybe pancakes with maple syrup in a diner somewhere. Do you like ice cream? Of course you do, everybody likes ice cream."

Trudi was gobsmacked as she finished reading Trevor's letter, her empty ice cream carton sat on her coffee table. How did he know?

It was almost 2:00 a.m. and she'd had a busy night, again. There was another Trevor in her circle who intruded her thoughts. A young, homeless, drug addict who had started to turn up for food most nights. It was hard to gauge his age, sixteen, seventeen? Skinny as a rake, dirty clothes, expressionless eyes and grey blotchy skin. She wondered if this Trevor was more lucky than her pen-pal Trevor, or were they both in similar boats, riding on parallel waves, cruising towards the same destination.

It was impossible to save them all, she was well aware, and indeed many didn't want to be helped, happy enough to receive a sleight of luck and be on their way. The world was full of losers.

23: A New Member in the Club

Earl Ryder was practically salivating upon hearing the news of a new addition to his walk. He'd been hoping the results would be in his favour after watching every bit of footage and news coverage of the case for months. It was that macabre not even the most prolific crime writer could make up.

Thirty-eight-year-old Ronnie Briggs and his fifty-two-year-old mother had both been awarded the ultimate prize - death by lethal injection, a sentence far too lenient in most people's estimation, considering the atrocities they'd committed on youngsters handed over to them to be cared for, nurtured, loved.

The whole country had been agog, disbelieving such things still happened in communities where authorities were supposed to keep check on young charges in care. Once again, the system had failed the fallen, the fragile and forgotten.

It was pathetic how remiss some of these so-called professionals carried out their commitments, how they would readily accept - on face value - the paltry excuses of the carers when explaining away the no show of the children.

Of course, they were always prepared for the visits of the governing bodies, having received prior notification, enough time to concoct plausible excuses AND ensure the rest of their charges adhered to the rules.

First it was thirteen-year-old Michael to disappear, then twelve-year-old Christopher. Georgia was also thirteen, Julia was nine. Jade was five and her sister, Pearl, three.

The case of this monstrous mother-and-son duo only surfaced because Jade and Pearl's mother managed to get her alcohol addiction under control, with a lot of help and support from her affluent family, and tried to get her children reinstated into her care, now that she was safely ensconced with her parents.

They had a wonderful, sprawling house set in two acres of idyllic pastures, ideal for a large family. It was a gloriously satisfying feeling for the grandparents to envision their new lives with a healthy daughter, albeit single, and their two much-loved granddaughters.

In preparing for their imminent arrival, a wing had been refurbished to accommodate all their requirements, as well as a mini play area outside. The grandparents had ensured both Ruby and granddaughters had their own personal space, their own cooking area and bathroom, bedrooms, etc., whilst feeling safe in the knowledge they could look out for them without encroaching on their privacy. It was an all-round ideal scenario. Or it would have been...

Ruby and her mother liaised totally with the Child Protective Services agents, eager to prove she was worthy to take her children back.

The agents were disappointed when they first arrived at the Briggs' home to discover the girls had 'gone away for the weekend with friends'. The following weekend was yet again a no-show. The whole place deserted.

Ruby was convinced the Briggs wanted to keep her daughters for themselves and she was equally convinced they wouldn't! She had appreciated the initial care when it was needed but now she had her own network of support and it was time for them to stand back and deliver her family.

The charred remains of three-year-old Pearl was found shackled to the body of her five-year-old sister, Jade, in a shallow fire pit that had piles of rocks on top. It was likely the pit had been used for many a barbecue after the girls' demise.

The decomposed and tortured bodies of Michael and Christopher were found in a makeshift grave at the bottom of a half-filled-in well. Julia's watery grave was a small lake that was a popular picnic and boating spot for locals. Georgia never left the house. Her naked body had been wrapped in garbage bin liners and kept in a locked freezer in the garage.

This despicable mother and son had managed to hoodwink neighbours and authorities for years, causing uproar in the community, leaving everyone to wonder how they got away with it! They outwardly appeared to be a pretty normal family. They were well dressed, articulate, and had a comfortable home with immaculate, sweeping gardens. Nothing out of the ordinary to raise any suspicion; in fact, neighbours had admired them for taking those children into their care, and had no reason to doubt anything sinister when one of them was no longer on the scene, assuming they had gone back to their own families.

Ruby and her mother's intervention brought the whole evilness to light when they were left with no alternative other than to seek a court order for the release of Jade and Pearl. It was harrowing news they received, and their lives went downhill rapidly, with Ruby's father suffering a fatal heart attack shortly after the discovery of his granddaughters. The funerals of three family members took place on a gloriously hot, sunny afternoon which felt like God was mocking them, it should have rained, the world should have been sad and full of gloom, the heavens should have cried.

Earl Ryder was going to make sure he could do everything in his power to avenge the murders of the pitiful kiddies and was going to take immense pleasure in doing so. He felt sure his colleagues would be on the same wavelength, nobody liked child killers, especially where they'd suffered horrifically by the hands of those who were supposed to care.

He thought back to his early years in the job, the days when that's all it was - a job; when he concluded even a man serving a life sentence deserved dignity in his final moments. It wasn't up to him to judge, that had already been done, and besides, a higher power altogether would make the ultimate judgement!

But children! No child should have to suffer, no matter what. The innocence of a child should be protected. They were supposed to only have good memories and people who abused that rule needed severe punishment, every second they were allowed to draw breath.

Gone were his days of playing by the book, a little fun would make the shift more enjoyable.

Ronnie Briggs was quite a debonair and charismatic man, but at only thirty-eight-years-old, he looked considerably older. He was nearing six-feet tall and his hair had greyed prematurely which gave him the appearance not of a son of his despicable mother, but could easily have been mistaken for her partner! In fact the relationship had been under scrutiny when it was revealed that he didn't have his own, separate bedroom and the crowds outside the courtroom hearings would be shouting 'Oedipus, Oedipus, give your mommy a kick from us'.

He paced his solitary cell, touching his single, utilitarian bed as if testing the mattress for comfort. He turned the faucet at the sink like he was in an hotel checking for faults. Earl was grinning like a Cheshire Cat, seeing the mighty fallen. It was incredibly satisfying to see the likes of inhumanity realising his destiny.

"Well, 'Train Robber', is everything to your satisfaction?" Ryder asked humorously, "or does one disapprove of the bed linen? Perhaps we can arrange for some nice Egyptian cotton ones to replace these used by your predecessor?"

"The water's cold." Briggs replied matter-of-factly.

"Oh, dearie me! Please accept my apologies on behalf of the management. I'll get maintenance on to it immediately. Will that be all, sir, or would you like me to send room service up with tonight's menu and the television guide?"

"Train robber? If I was a train robber I would be living comfortably in some exotic country."

"Well now, the smarter Ronnie *Biggs* did, didn't he. Similar names, same ending. I think the name 'Train

Robber' will suffice as a suitable nickname. Pity you didn't get the same lucky break, hey? But I guess the Englishman was never despised as much as you. Some thought him quite lucrative, in fact. Perhaps your mother admired him, too, and that's why she named you after him?"

"I'm guessing you love your job, I bet…"

"Oh, I do, sir! I do love my job. I love all the residents here, I get really emotional when it's time for goodbyes, knowing we're never going to enjoy our daily banter again and losing that… well, not *friendship* exactly; *camaraderie*." Earl chuckled, "That um, how would one describe it? The familiarity, I suppose. Yes, that's the word, familiarity. Like 'family' really. Yes, I thoroughly enjoy working with my 'family' here and you know what families are like don't you, sir? Hah, well, you can pick your friends but you can't pick your family. Perhaps you might consider yourself amongst a new family. After all, you're all in the same place, destined for the same final destination, and you can share each other's sunscreen cos I hear it's scorching hot where you're all going!"

Earl removed the man's shackles, cuffs, and restraints whilst his colleague waited to lock the cell door. Brown and Cave has been pressed up against their own doors to try to hear what was going on close by. As the screws walked by, they stopped to impart a little gossip, "…killed six kids as far we know... God knows how many others. From now on he will be referred to as 'The Train Robber'."

"The 'Train Robber'? He murdered six children and they class him as a train robber? I don't get it," said Trevor.

Cole didn't get it either but then, who knew how the minds of the screws worked? You had to be a bordering psycho to want to be in their profession.

"Poor kids," whispered Trevor, "I wonder why he killed them…"

"It doesn't matter does it? They're dead, perhaps a good thing," Cole commented dryly.

"What? A good thing? How can a kid being dead be a good thing? A kid is just a kid, they don't do anything bad enough to warrant being killed, for God's sake. What planet are you on Caveman? Would you kill a kid, or have you?"

"I meant 'a good thing' as at least they're at peace, spared anything further from the hands of evil."

"Oh, yes, I see what you're saying, slightly. Perhaps death was a better life - or whatever. I don't know though. You know, sometimes death isn't the better alternative cos children are resilient and they get over stuff, traumas and bad things that happen to them. They forget or choose not to remember. I remember once, when I was little, my mother took the stick to me because I called her a cow, but I didn't mean she was a cow in a bad way, it was because she was breastfeeding my sister, like a cow would suckle a calf. But she made welts on my legs and I couldn't sit down properly for days. I cursed her for hurting me because it wasn't necessary, that whipping. She just misunderstood me."

"That tells me how stupid your mother was…"

"Oh no, she apologised afterwards, once she realised what I was trying to say, you see…"

"No, stop interrupting. Your mother was stupid that she didn't whip you into shape. 'Spare the rod, spoil the child' and that's where she went wrong. She didn't discipline you adequately and that's why you're here now, boring the ass off me. If she'd been a decent mother, taught you right from wrong, you'd be a nice man outside living a decent life. She failed you as a mother."

Trevor felt irritated with Cole's wrongly assumed analysis of his mother, how dare he!

"*Touché*. 'He who liveth in glass houses should not throw stones'. What's your excuse? Let me guess? You were a big mistake and your underage mother had been badgered into an abortion, which she would later come to regret not having, but… she decided anyway to go ahead and give birth to you, having no idea how she was going to make ends meet."

Trevor's evisceration continued, "She lived in a trailer, probably selling herself for a dollar or two just to keep you in diapers and a few fancy pieces of underwear to lure her next score… I bet you were taken into care and rebelled cos you missed your *mommy*. Boo hoo. Bet she was glad to get rid of the burden of you! It enabled her the freedom to entertain all those men."

If only he knew, thought Cole. He couldn't be further from the truth if he tried.

"Spot on. Our mothers were both whores. Tell me a female that isn't?"

Trevor wanted to contradict him. He wanted to say a queen bee wasn't a whore, but that alone in the very science of beekeeping wasn't the truth. The queen bee *was* nothing less than a whore! And he knew it was only the female bees that stung. He suddenly remembered reading that only a few female species were totally monogamous, such as swans, lobsters, and many birds. He hated to consider the possibility that perhaps Cole was right after all.

"Hello!" a voice echoed down the walk, "how many are here? Can anyone actually hear me?"

"Cole, is that 'The Train Robber'? Are you gonna answer him?"

"You're the gob on a stick, why don't you?"

"I can't! You're the murderer here, not me! I've got nothing I want to say to him."

"Then he's gonna be blessed he's not living next door to you."

"Hello! I said, 'can anyone hear me?'."

"Ignore him or we'll never hear the last of him," whispered Trevor.

"*YES*, motherfucker, loud and clear, unfortunately," Cole shouted back, "forgive our rude welcome but we're kinda anti-social in this neighbourhood, unless you have alcohol or smokes, then you're welcome to join the party."

"Well, I'm not gonna to acknowledge him. I've a letter to answer."

Dear Mr Hansome

Many thanks for your letter. Yes, of course I would be delighted to meet with Ms Hopkins.

As you are aware, my social calendar is pretty empty so any time would be great. I'm sure Warden Statham will liaise with you and notify you of a convenient date.

I am most grateful to be afforded this privilege.

Yours sincerely,

Trevor Brown

8356

"She's requested a visit," Trevor said just above a whisper.

Cole nodded. He'd expected something like this, sooner or later. "I want a full description and leave nothing out. I want to know what the lovely Ms Hopkins looks like, smells like, feels like."

Trevor gasped in surprise, "Will I be able to actually touch her?"

"You will be sat behind a screen in a tiny booth with just a telephone receiver to talk to her. Use your imagination kid. Take in the scene and paint me the image so that I can dream of her. Tell me the colour of her eyes, her hair and skin. Look at her teeth and listen closely to every word she says. Watch her body language, the way she uses her hands to touch her face and neck because she will. They're so easy to read, once you know their language. You won't get to smell her perfume – but tell her you can and that she smells like a goddess, and close your eyes when you tell her that, like you're inhaling her."

"I will do no such thing, I'm not a damn pervert! She's a pen-pal and she's requested a visit, which is more than most have done since I've been here. I'm not about to disillusion her, you fool. I think she may be able to help me once she actually gets to meet me and ask my story. Do you think she might ask me about my story? She hasn't so far."

"I've no doubt she knows every solitary thing about you, right down to your shoe size. These broads get a kick out of bad guys. It's in their maternal make-up. Use it to your advantage, feed her lust."

"I don't think Trudi is like the female species you seem to be familiar with. She's had her own amount of bad luck but she's – "

"Ah! I see! She's already embroidered her own sorry state of woebegone. Hah! Oh boy, you're on a loser already, kid. No way are you gonna get her to listen to you. You're gonna want to end up silencing her sorry self. Okay, just agree to the visit and keep picturing her naked. At least you'll get a satisfactory night's sleep!"

Cole chuckled for several minutes afterwards, loud enough to piss Trevor off and silent enough to disguise his jealousy.

24: Warden Statham

Warden Statham was greatly disappointed. He'd been harbouring a liking for 5216 ever since he came to be under his jurisdiction. Cave's aloofness was almost an air of gratitude for his fate, something Statham rarely witnessed. He'd been the model prisoner, never making demands, never raising objections…

It was inevitable that personalities mattered in such circumstances, because of course it did, in every circle of life. Personalities could make or break any human-being, could enrich or destroy a person. Having good looks as well as a good personality would be the icing on the cake, such as Cave had had once upon-a-time, as a young man. Judging a book by its cover was par for the course in life. One rarely read between the lines or looked beyond the façade. Most people really are shallow.

Statham had now seen beyond the façade. He'd read and reread everything there was to know about the multi-faceted 'Caveman' and his empathy vanished. He dictated a memo to his secretary to set up a meeting with the governor explaining the need to free up a couple of cells on the walk. It was time to show the State that they were not dragging their heels in acquiescing to their judicial obligations. The public needed to be appeased.

25: The Visit

Trevor was anxious. He wanted to make a good impression for Trudi because it was his first visitor since his incarceration.

He'd showered and shaved. He'd drawn up a list of questions he wanted to ask her and answers to questions he hoped she would ask of him.

He remembered Cole telling him to remember the smell of her, to take in the clothes she'd be wearing; what she looked like and everything she said. He wanted to do all of that, but it was going to be for his benefit only. He was going to enjoy his moment without sharing a minute.

And there she was, sitting behind the Perspex screen just as Cole has described, smiling as she watched him walk up and sit down opposite her. He said 'hello' and she laughed as she picked up the telephone receiver, nodding for him to do likewise.

"Hello, Trudi. Thank you for coming to see me. You have no idea how happy I've been since I learned I was going to have a visitor. How are you?"

"Nice to meet you, Trevor, at long last. It's good to put a face to the man I've been talking to over these last months. I've thoroughly enjoyed our letter writing, backwards and forwards. You make me laugh. That's why I wanted to come over and meet you."

"Are you wearing perfume? I ask because I can't smell anything on this side, so I need to imagine it."

"Oh, well, actually, no, I'm not. I don't usually bother with such things as expensive toiletries because in my line of work I feel it's exploiting my freedom because of course those I help can't afford such luxuries. I usually smell of cooked burgers or onion soup. Not very flattering I assure you."

"Burgers and onions, I can imagine that," he laughed. "I love your letters, too! I read them over and over. They give me a reason to smile and something to look forward to."

"Elaine has asked me to send you her best regards, by the way. You remember she was the one who suggested I write to you?"

Trevor nodded. It was difficult trying to converse through a screen, on the end of a telephone, but at least they were able to see each other.

"Tell me all about your food kitchen. I know you've told me in your letters, but I'd like you to tell me in more detail. What made you decide to help those people out on the streets and what are their alternatives if you weren't there?"

Trudi looked into Trevor's eyes, "Trevor, they would eventually cease to exist, probably. For most, my food franchise is a last and only resort. They're on a downward spiral, nothing to look forward to. Somewhat similar to your situation I imagine. Your saving grace is that you do have sustenance on a regular basis, you have your health needs addressed, and you – "

Trevor smiled, not wanting to disillusion her. "That's true, Trudi, we do. I am lucky in that respect. I want for nothing here, apart from redemption, of course, which I'm working on constantly. I'm writing a book; did I tell you?"

"You mentioned something about writing something but I don't think you actually said it was a book. What kind of book is it?"

"It's the truth, Trudi. I've already decided on the title and I'm going to tell it all, because if it's there in black and white then people have to take notice, don't they? They can't ignore the facts."

"Honey, didn't the jury listen to the facts? You know, at your trial?"

Trevor didn't miss that term of endearment *'honey'.*

The alarm sounded, announcing they had two more minutes. Trevor was grief-stricken: the time had flown and they both had so much more to say.

"I've always hated bells and alarm clocks," Trudi said softly into the mouthpiece, "they're a reminder that we're all governed by time. It goes so quickly and yet I'm sure for someone in your position that isn't the case."

"They heard a lot of misinformation which they assumed to be facts. I'm a young black man. These prisons are full of men like me," he said in his eagerness to keep their earlier conversation on track. "Trudi, I wouldn't waste yours or anyone's time on someone here if I didn't think I was worth it. I promise you, I'm not the evil person I've been portrayed as. If you will allow me, I'd like to send you some chapters of my manuscript…"

The telephone connection went silent. All lines were disconnected and it was time for visitors to leave. Trudi smiled and mouthed that she would write soon. She stood up, hauling her crocheted handbag over her shoulder, saddened to see Trevor being manhandled, manacled, and manoeuvred from his chair.

It was easy for her, she realised. She had the freedom and funds to do exactly as she pleased, every minute of the day. She answered to nobody and vice versa. She was getting back into a taxi to take her home to the comfort of her own four walls and sanctuary where she could indulge herself any which way she desired. That was her routine, the way she passed her time. Invariably there were certain people she encountered who tore at her heart strings and made way into her night-time thoughts, such as the Trevor she knew. But "black Trevor', or 'death row Trevor' occupied most.

Trudi liked him. She enjoyed their banter, and had he been just that tad older she had no doubt that she could find herself daydreaming about being more than just a pen-pal, but pen-pals they were. There was so much to learn.

"Well? What did she smell like, tell me. Did she wear lipstick and eye laggy?"

"Eye laggy? Do you mean make-up? No, she didn't. Didn't need to, she was beautiful without the need for all that warpaint."

Cole waited for 'mouth almighty' to expand on his visit, to give him something to comfort him when the lights went out that night.

"And?"

"Oh you wanna talk now? Sorry, but our conversation was private, you understand. Excuse me but I have some writing to do. Good night."

26: Alice

Alice was just a couple of weeks younger than Trevor Brown. She lived in the same vicinity, attended the same class at the same school. She'd always had a secret admiration for him. She loved to listen to his many stories, finding most of them hilarious!

Invariably, Trevor would have an audience during break times when he would talk of his beekeeping and his aspirations of becoming an astronaut. He would captivate his school pals with his wit and knowledge and loved to answer any question thrown his way. The playground became a stage on which he would perform to their bidding.

These were the moments when school appealed to him and felt it worthwhile attending. To show off his expertise in subjects that his peers could only wonder about, he glorified his answers, going to great lengths in his descriptions of his hobby and his ambition. He would role-play, act, embellish, enthralling not only Alice but the many without the same attributes he possessed.

She was a sweet-faced girl with shoulder-length blonde hair and a face full of pale freckles that made her look fairy-like, destined to be a stunner when she reached adulthood. By the time Trevor reached his seventeenth birthday, Alice and Trevor were considered a 'couple' in the eyes of their circle of friends. Anne, Trevor's mother, had no idea of her son's friendship with the opposite sex, or his secret night-time rendezvous.

It wasn't really a case of Trevor being secretive, more a case of shyness in the admissible realisation of 'growing up', the things an adolescent tries to keep under wraps from nosy parents. It felt like a taboo subject to discuss with his mother and in front of his younger sister, who would undoubtedly tease him unmercifully. He did, however, confide in Jonah, the man he considered a steadfast father-figure.

Jonah had always been there to lend a listening ear, a shoulder to cry on, a pillar of strength to lean on. Jonah was kind, caring, strong and supportive, and Trevor aspired to be like him.

Alice's family background wasn't dissimilar to Trevor's in that neither was very affluent. However, she did have four brothers that looked out for her, Rocky – the eldest – more so than the others. Miles, the second eldest, was blind so he had no understanding of his brothers' reluctance to allow their sister's friendship with their black neighbour. They grew up together, played together, learned together. So as far as Miles was concerned, what did colour matter? He could only judge on actions and feelings: visual matters were immaterial and he'd tried endlessly to get his point of view to his blinkered brothers.

Miles would often reiterate the teachings of the pastor from their Sunday morning church attendances; 'Do not judge by appearances, but judge with right judgment.' The words of wisdom spoken by their mother - 'never judge a book by its cover'. For Miles, this was easy, he had no preconceived picture in his mind because he had never seen. Miles 'felt' people, spiritually, mentally, and physically. That's how he would make his observations of a person. He couldn't understand how it wasn't the same simple and obvious way for everyone.

Skin was skin. Fur and feathers the same. He was confused when his mother bought beef from the supermarket, or lamb, pork, chicken, but a dog or a cat was a family pet and any killing or harming of such animals was considered an outrage! He couldn't understand the fundamental differences.

Rocky, Trevor, Alice, and so many others grew up together. Why did his brother feel so aggrieved that the two were becoming an item? When did it change from being acceptable as friends, to unacceptable as a couple?

Rocky had tried to tell his brother over and over that their sister shouldn't be lowering her standards: she deserved a lot better than a black boy with no prospects. Miles had no conception of black or white. He had been told he lived in a world of darkness where everything was black, but in his mind, in *his* black world, that was normal. Colours were just words he heard.

He remembered his mother, years ago, trying to describe colours to him, to associate them with certain things. She would pour cold water over his hands and explain that the water was crystal clear, colourless. What did colourless mean? It made no sense. The sun, beaming its hot rays on his tender skin, was yellow. A citrus orange fruit, was orange. The bitter taste of a lemon that made one screw up their mouth in horror, was lemon, and also yellow like the sun. Grass was green and so was envy and ignorance.

Miles found it incredibly mind-blowing to wonder how sighted people could learn to assimilate everything. Colours represented a whole different kind of vocabulary for him.

A rainbow – of which he could never get his head around – was a multi coloured arc. Fire was yellow, amber, red – along with anger and embarrassment. Sad was blue, like the oceans and sky. God was a glowing bright light, like the moon and stars. Miles preferred to use his own imagination for colours, just different shades of black and white.

He made his family wear blindfolds on occasions so that they could glimpse into his dark world. He would ask them to walk to the kitchen, get the potato peeler from the table drawer and peel a potato or carrot. Then he'd get them to fill the kettle to make a cup of coffee, making them put their fingers at the top of the cup to feel the hot water fill up. His siblings would laugh when the game extended to eating from plates in front of them because it was impossible for them to use cutlery when they couldn't see the food, resulting in them having to use their fingers to feed themselves. Food would be all over the place and everyone would end up in hysterics.

It was fun, and it was funny for his family who were able to emerge from the obscurity of a blindfold and carry out simple tasks effortlessly. Not so for Miles who would forever live in a world of darkness.

No, he decided, Rocky was so wrong. A person should be judged on their character, their deeds, not by visual appearances. He liked Trevor, he loved to listen to his witticisms and his tantalising stories. He found it fascinating that the buzzing insects he talked of were essential for the whole world's fruit and vegetable production, without which the planet would cease to exist. He had no idea that bees pollinated practically everything they ate and marvelled that such a tiny creature had so much worldly value.

He never exactly envied sighted people because he knew no other, in fact he considered he was better off being blind than deaf, like a cousin of theirs. At least Miles was able to join in family conversations, he could distinguish the birds by their calls and songs. He could dance to music by feeling the beat, sing hymns at church, hear the kettle switch off and the microwave ping. The weather fascinated him when he felt the cool wind whip round him yet couldn't feel it in his hands; the warmth of the sun creating blisters and sweat on his body. Why did the heavens crack and shudder when thunderstorms erupted, which used to unnerve him as a small child, crying out in terror for his mother who would pacify him in her reassurance that it was a natural occurrence the world over?

Miles was unseeing yet had the ability to 'view' things differently from the rest of his family, and that included his insight into the Alice and Trevor situation. From his stance, there was no problem, hence he could never share his brother's angst over their liaison.

He remembered that night vividly, the night it all happened. He didn't want to be involved, but Rocky had insisted all the brothers rally together, telling them they needed to do this to protect their sister, and whilst Miles had argued that Alice was more than capable of choosing her own friends, like them, she was doing nothing wrong. What was so wrong with their sister having Trevor as a boyfriend? Not one of his brothers found anything derogatory to say about him other than he was black and Alice was white and they needed to prevent any further involvement between them. Rocky was steadfast that they needed to step up to 'protect' their younger sister and do his bidding. They were forbidden to tell a soul!

Rocky had been practically stalking Alice for months, watching her sneak out of the house at night to meet Trevor. He'd waited outside Trevor's house, too, seeing him climb out of his sister's bedroom and scurrying off to their rendezvous. He'd watched in fury as the love-struck teens kissed and canoodled together, walked hand-in-hand at the back of the beehives and secretively listened to Trevor glorify his tales and ambitions.

The times he'd wanted to leap out and surprise the two, thump the living daylights out of the boy who had captured his sister's heart, and felt an insatiable feeling of frustration.

Was it a feeling of over-protectiveness or was it jealousy? He didn't question it, he just knew he had to end it, and soon!

Rocky had decided when and planned every detail. He now knew his sister's movements and when he heard her bedroom window open, he got his brothers together. It was perfect. Their mother had gone to visit a friend and wouldn't be back until very late. By then, everything would be settled. Life, as he wanted it again, would be hunky-dory.

27: Trudi

After her visit, Trudi wanted to know everything about Trevor and the reasons for his incarceration. For weeks she had put off doing any Google searches because she wanted to form her own unbiased opinion, even though that was nigh on impossible considering where he was!

She was no stranger to hearing sob stories; she encountered them every day of her life. She had witnessed those lost souls who had nothing, meandering around in a fog of despair, losing the will to live. Nobody could save everybody, but she knew she was doing her bit to get at least some to see the beginning of a brand new day.

Becoming acquainted with Trevor had given her another angle to channel her thoughts and generosity. Besides, Trevor wasn't at all like the down-and-outs she helped, Trevor was articulate and amusing.

She recalled one of his letters in which he wrote about his image of Heaven, should he fail in his attempt at redemption and his sentence be carried out. He assured her he would most definitely go to Heaven because Hell was only for the wicked and the non-believers. He described Heaven as just another planet in the galaxy where all the dead people and animals finally rested. The good ones, he assured her. All the others went to the sun, which was Hell.

'Can you imagine, Trudi, I will get to meet my hero - Neil Armstrong - and, of course, my kin. You see, God knows, doesn't he? He knows the truth about everyone because he watches over us all. Heaven must be an enormous planet to accommodate all the dead people and animals that have died since the beginning of time. There will be dinosaurs and extinct animals, vast oceans for the dolphins, whales, and all marine life. Forests for wolves and birds, lions and elephants. It's hard to picture isn't it, Heaven?'

Only Trevor could talk about dinosaurs walking around in Heaven!

Elaine topped up their glasses of Rioja; the second bottle was almost empty.

"The 'Death-Rowers' aren't there for no reason, Trudi. A jury had to listen and see a mountain of evidence before their deliberation and they rarely get it wrong. Matthew's not stupid, either, and he was his attorney. He hates to lose a case."

"So did Matt think he was guilty?"

"I'm just his secretary and PA, a glorified typist in other words. He's fed up with the constant barrage of pleading letters from him. He has to believe in the innocence of all his clients, otherwise how can he defend them so passionately?"

"Money?"

"Not in Trevor Brown's case. They didn't have any. His mother had to sell their home to pay his legal fees. I heard she's now living in a trailer somewhere. From what I can remember - from the notes I typed - Trevor raped and murdered his girlfriend in a frenzied attack. Then he went on to kill his mother's boyfriend by overturning his beehives. He was a beekeeper, see: so was Trevor, so he'd know exactly what he was doing. Can't quite understand why he went on to kill his mother's boyfriend because according to the transcripts, Trevor idolised him. It was the boyfriend who'd taught him everything there was to know about beekeeping. Guess you can never know what's inside a twisted mind, hey?"

"That's what I don't understand, Elaine. Trevor doesn't seem to have a twisted mind. His is more of a curious mind, not cruel or vindictive. He's almost naive in a lot of ways. I can't imagine him killing a fly let alone another person. Beekeepers are usually phlegmatic individuals who are emphatic about preserving the future of productivity, not necessarily in the Biblical sense, but you get my gist?"

"I've never met the guy so can't really – "

"He's cute, I tell ya. If I was a few years younger, I tell you, I would!"

The two friends fell about laughing, recalling their weekend shenanigans when drink would have them in hysterics over the simplest things.

"And another thing," Elaine continued, "don't forget that these guys will lie through their back teeth to a sympathetic audience. They'll tell you what they think you want to hear. I'm not going to try to convince you not to believe in him because that's up to you, but just because he tells you he's innocent doesn't mean he is. Read what you can about him, if you want to know all the dirt, but it's not pretty reading."

Trudi drove home that night determined to learn more about the young man she was writing to and getting to know. Would her opinion change? Would she still want to be his friend once the stark evidence stared her in the face? Elaine's parting words, *"it's not pretty reading,"* echoing in her thoughts.

She shuddered as she realised she'd deliberately failed to acknowledge Trevor could have committed such heinous crimes, choosing to view him through rose-coloured glasses as, indeed, his victims must have done. Wouldn't it be an easy world to live in, she considered, if all the evil people were instantly recognisable and thus one was able to avoid?

But not all killers are evil. Many crimes are committed on the spur of the moment, crimes of passion, or by accident. Trudi was of the opinion that everybody was capable of murder, given certain circumstances. She herself had experienced the feeling of wanting to avenge her own parents' death at the time, but surely that was a natural reaction, feeling angry and bitter, wanting someone to blame and pay for the overwhelming suffering she was enduring.

Why had no one been indicted for the deaths of her parents? Why weren't alcohol producers put behind bars for the loss of lives due to alcoholism? Bath, staircase, window manufactures for the obvious accidents that result in a death?

Who decides that an accident resulting in a death is unworthy of a prison sentence when a person has been killed? When does a killer become less guilty than a murderer? Trudi played around with the words in her head as she continued her homeward journey. Killer versus murderer. Where does the division begin and end?

She arrived outside her apartment just before midnight. The full moon was eerily bright and, bar the sound of the odd vehicle passing, all seemed exceptionally quiet. She parked in her designated spot and turned her ignition key off, listening to the clicking sound as the engine settled down. There was a strangeness about this particular night; something didn't 'feel' quite right.

Before she got out of her car, she looked around and noticed something propped up against the wall of her apartment. It resembled a heap of dumped rubbish, which dismayed her. Why did people just dump their trash when there were dumpsters everywhere?

Trudi cautiously locked her car and was walking apprehensively to her door when she stopped dead in her tracks. She recognised the gaunt grey-faced young drug addict… Trevor number 2.

She had no idea how long the boy had been dead or why he was outside her home. She sat with him, cuddling him, stroking his greasy, matted hair, and whispering kind words until the police and ambulance arrived. Her tears had cleaned parts of his face, making a mockery of his stolen youthfulness for he looked clown-like.

Trudi was consumed by guilt, feeling that he had sought her out for some kind of salvation that she wasn't able to fulfill. If only she hadn't gone over to Elaine's, or if she'd returned earlier… Those mental 'what ifs' again were purgatory.

As drug addict Trevor's lifeless body was taken away, she sat down in the same position he had occupied and sobbed, knowing he deserved at least someone's tears. The police and ambulance crew would have no such emotion for what they considered a waste of time and resources. There were far too many to be sympathetic.

Life counts for nothing in some cases. Meaningless, futile, worthless. Who cares, who *really* cares? Trudi witnessed a young boy being placed in a body bag and whisked away to a morgue by people who were supposed to be pillars of the caring community but failed to see any, assuming a drug addict had his comeuppance, his just desert, 'got what he wanted', et cetera…

She had decided right there and then that the young Trevor number 2 would have a proper funeral. She'd ensure that his life was respected, be damned to the high and mighty who thought otherwise.

Dear Trevor,

It was wonderful to finally meet you last week and eventually put a face and voice to your letters. Are you up for another rendezvous soon? I'm in need of some alternative conversation. I'm going to submit a request today and hope that's OK with you.

Kind regards,

Trudi"

Trevor's response was, she thought, quite elegant and eloquent:

Trudi! Why so formal? Of course, it's OK! You're my reason to smile every morning, my reason to piss off my neighbour because he gets no one writing or visiting him, but please don't think my corresponding with you is just a ploy to piss him off, because it isn't. It's my own pure selfishness.

There is no such thing as friendship here. It's purely an outlet to vent our spleen or just pour out anything that's in our heads to a listening ear. Not that there are willing listening ears: we have no choice. A new arrival we call 'The Train Robber', constantly calls out to us, but we don't acknowledge him because we've been told he's a child killer and nobody wants to converse or give the time of day to the likes of someone like that.

I talk to Cole because he's next door. He tolerates me, most of the time. Ever since I've been here, I've talked to him. He's familiar now. Sometimes he says profound things and it's almost as if we actually know each other, but the truth is, Trudi, he hates me more than I dislike him.

It's funny, isn't it, how you can feel you know someone without actually seeing them. We see the screws when they bring our food. We see the auxiliaries when they take us to shower… ordinary guys you'd probably see in the supermarkets when you do your shopping, never questioning what they do for a living, how they while away their hours before going home to their families, gathering round the dining table to eat before settling on the sofa to watch the television. I wonder if they tell their wives about us here. You know, do they actually admit to spitting in our food, pulling out a piece of bread from their underwear and expect us to eat it? Of course they don't! It's all fun for them, to taunt and ridicule; we're a big joke to them.

They love being our intended executioners, it goes towards feeding their morbid desire of empowerment. They're basically legalised killers - 'Licensed to Kill' - but because it's a job, they get to wander freely on the other side of the bars. Strange, isn't it, don't you think?"

Trudi drew a sharp breath. This was the very same subject she was talking to herself about! Was this guy on her wavelength or what?

She laughed to herself, thinking of the many times he'd written about subjects that made her gasp, nod her head in agreement, and making her reach out for her pen and notepad to write back quickly. How could he possibly be guilty of such despicable crimes?

"And another thing, don't forget that these guys will lie through their back teeth to a sympathetic audience."

"Damn you, Elaine. I hope everybody is wrong. I AM going to Google his case now, and I will listen to him."

It was eight in the morning when she realised she'd not gone to bed after reading everything she could find about Trevor Carlton Brown. It had now become personal, and she wanted to invest as much time as she could to enable her to make her own judgement.

She called her colleague to ask him to recruit reinforcements for the food kitchen, explaining that she wouldn't be available for a while – possibly two or three weeks – reiterating that she was making plans for the other Trevor's funeral arrangements. She wanted to keep focused, to try to remain impartial, scrutinising and dissecting every statement.

She was amazed to find so much detail of the court case available to the general public and dismayed to see so much incriminating evidence stacked against him. It was deflating to acknowledge that her friend was rotten to the core after all.

She sat at her PC staring at the screen, her cup of coffee gone cold next to it, sympathising with Alice's blind brother, Miles, being dragged into his brother's vendetta.

Being an only child, Trudi had no conception of sibling loyalties, nor could she comprehend Rocky's disdain for his sister's relationship with Trevor purely because of his skin colour. Surely that type of prejudice went out with the ark?

'I heard a grunting sound. You know, like sex sounds. I may not be able to see but there's nothing wrong with my hearing. I knew what was happening.'

So Miles, the blind brother, testified to hearing his sister being raped?

'And then I heard a clicking noise. Click, click, click, click. Like the shutter of a camera lens. That slow scratchy sound.'

What was that clicking sound Miles had heard? There was no reference after that statement. Why did Alice not say anything? If she was being raped, why was she not screaming out? The only answer Trudi could assume was that Alice wasn't being raped, or was she forcibly silenced, gagged? But even so, she would've been able to make some sort of sound.

Were her brothers watching and she had no idea? What was Miles not saying? Was Rocky or someone else taking photographs of the young lovers, and that was the clicking sound he heard? If so, where were those photographs?

Trudi felt that Miles had witnessed a whole lot more than his non-seeing eyes foretold.

Sibling loyalty can be priceless; parental loyalty too. In fact, Trudi was beginning to wonder what was truth and what wasn't. She was willing and capable enough to believe everyone, never analysing further than necessary.

She began to realise the pressure of her friend's employer, Matt, who *had* to analyse every minute detail, go through every statement with a fine-tooth comb, sifting through chaff and grain. It must be an enormous responsibility, she decided, for every legal team, forensics, pathologists, judges, jurors... The list was endless.

It was no wonder errors were made in the final decision because who goes through their lives and careers without making a single mistake? In her own humble vocation, it was no big deal. If she'd not prepared enough food for one night or hadn't distributed adequate bedding, no one would be suing the pants off her. Her insurance premium wouldn't skyrocket. Her clientele were simply very grateful for everything she did for them.

How she would love to get access to Trevor's case files because there was only so much one could find on the internet.

She'd already posted her request to the warden for a follow-up visit and had compiled a list of questions she was going to ask Trevor. She wanted to believe in his proclamations of innocence, even though Elaine's words continued to haunt her.

As a child, her father would read her bedtime stories, her favourite was Aesop's Fables. She knew them all, practically by heart. They made her lay awake for hours dissecting the logic until finally understanding the meanings.

It was The Scorpion and the Frog story she recalled. The scorpion asked a frog to carry him across the river. The frog was afraid of being stung, but the scorpion explained that if he did that, both would die and the scorpion would drown. So the frog agreed, but halfway across the river the scorpion did sting the frog, dooming them both. The frog asked why the scorpion would break his promise knowing they'd both die. To which the scorpion replied, "I couldn't help it, it's in my nature."

'It's in my nature' she remembered. Those words! It was nothing at all to do with nurture, it's purely and simply nature!

A killer *is* born, and would show signs from an early age, she assumed. There was no such incriminating background info on Trevor. On the contrary, his school reports were glowing with teachers extolling his many virtues, including empathy for his fellow school chums.

He was a beekeeper who was fastidious with their care. He had a lovely girlfriend for whom he cared deeply and she him. He had no reason to rape or kill her because Alice's mother had testified to her willingness to consummate their relationship.

And Jonah: the man he regarded as a mentor and father-figure. Why would he want to hurt him, or - penultimately - his mother?

Why then, was her friend on death row?

28: Trudi's Second Meeting With Trevor

It was the same set-up as their previous meeting, both behind a thick Perspex screen. Trudi had cleared the security screening and was led to her allocated kiosk. He was already sitting there, attired as she remembered from their first visit, grinning like an expectant child at the circus waiting for the performers to strut their stuff.

She couldn't contain her gleeful smile back as she chuckled when picking up the handset, "I'd like to break into song about how good it is to see you again, Trevor, but we have limited time and I want to ask many questions before I get chucked out of here, so are you OK with me firing questions at you?"

He nodded in confusion, wondering where her questioning was going.

"OK," she said, "we write and talk in our letters and have great conversations, yes?"

Trevor nodded.

"I've been reading about you." She studied his face, waiting to see a reaction, which lit up expectantly

"Then you believe me! You know."

"No, Trevor, no. It's not that simple, honey." (Again, that 'honey' reference he noticed.). "Hey, I wasn't there, I've – "

"Trudi, I wasn't there either. I swear to you. I'm incapable of committing the crimes I've been accused of. If you've been reading about me, you'll know to what I'm referring, but ask yourself why would I hurt the two people who meant the world to me? Alice was my lifelong girlfriend. Jonah was like my father. He loved me and my family. I had no reason to end either of their lives. None! *Comprende?* Please don't come here and sit before me and tell me you are having doubts because if that's the case then let's call it a day because I'm already surrounded by people who have decided my guilt."

Trudi was downhearted. She hadn't intended the conversation to take a spiral decline so quickly, or the sudden self-defensive attitude.

"Trevor, I haven't decided any such thing. I just – "

"Just what? Want more proof? I'm not able to do that, am I? Everything was read out in the court and the evidence was stacked against me. My semen was found on Alice. The jury *assumed* I killed her afterwards. Why would I have wanted to do that? And then Jonah. They again *assumed* I'd gone on a killing spree and destroyed his bee hives. The bee hives that I helped him with. Jonah was a decent man and my family loved him. They all *assumed* wrongly, Trudi, because to assume only makes an *ass* out of *u* and *me*."

Trudi said nothing. She was cautious about asking anything further, hoping he would calm down.

Eventually, she dared to speak. "I know," she said, softly. 'They were my thoughts too. It makes no sense. That's why I'd like to try to help you, if you will allow me. Trevor. I came here today to try to get some information from you so that I can... I don't know, possibly find something that was overlooked, missed, and if so, then surely we can get a retrial, or at least a stay of execution?"

Trevor was frowning, it wasn't the enjoyable reunion he'd been anticipating.

She continued, "Miles, the blind brother, said – "

"He wasn't there. He was lying. All the brothers were lying. When Alice and I left, we both got dressed and kissed each other goodnight. I left first because it was getting late, and I'd left my sister's bedroom window unlocked. I didn't want to worry her because she felt unsafe with it that way. Alice was very much alive when I kissed her goodbye."

Trudi nodded, making mental notes, trying to absorb as much information as she could. "Well, somebody knew the two of you were there, and had probably been watching."

"Dirty perverts," Trevor scowled.

"Who would want Jonah dead?" she asked.

"Nobody. He was the nicest man I've ever known. Everybody liked him. As far as I know, no one had a bad word to say against him. He was very kind to us. He taught me everything there is to know about beekeeping and set me up with my own hives. He liked his photography, too. He was good at it. Could've made a living as a professional photographer, but he lacked ambition. Besides," he shrugged dismissively, "it was just another hobby."

"Photography?" Something resonated in her memory box.

Trevor smiled, remembering the time they discovered the dead golden retriever hanging in the waitress's campervan, just before his sister's birthday. He'd tried to coerce Jonah into taking a photograph of it, but Jonah was repulsed and refused.

"A Canon. Digital. He prints them too. Sorry - printed them. Past tense. His living room walls were full of various photos. I bet they all ended up in the trash when they cleared everything out and sold his property. I spent many happy times at his place. I hope my mother was given something of his."

"Would you like me to find out? Shall I pay her a visit?"

Trevor's face creased in confusion. "Can you do that? I mean, do you know where they are? I heard that she sold our home to pay my legal costs and I don't know where they went afterwards. Didn't do much good, did it? Seems even my own mother *assumes* I did it."

Trudi felt genuine pity for the young man behind the Perspex screen. If he *was* as innocent as he proclaimed, it was immensely unjust.

The bell blasted on cue, reminding visitors that their time was up, but Trudi had one more pressing question. "Your sister, Eva? How old was she when –"

The line went dead. That was it. No further communication was allowed. She mouthed to him "Write soon." He nodded.

29: Trudi's Visit to Anne

Trudi had a hell of a job locating Anne. She'd had to resort to begging Elaine for an address, with Elaine making her swear never to disclose where the information came from. Trudi quickly learned that trailer parks in Georgia were not the most luxurious places to live, but what alternative did Anne have?

Trudi knocked tentatively on the trailer door, pleasantly surprised to see sparkling windows with pretty lace net curtains at the window, then was bowled over when a very elegant, beautiful young black woman answered.

It was Friday, midday. Trudi felt confident Anne would be alone, assuming her daughter would be in school, and at the same time daunted as to how she would be received once she explained the reason for her visit. She needn't have been so apprehensive because Anne was over the moon for a friend of her son to visit, enabling her the exceedingly rare opportunity to talk about him in a positive light.

Trudi gave Anne a quick synopsis of her visit, then proceeded to reveal her life history, feeling a great warmth and comfort from this lady.

The two sympathised with each other's tales of woe, and several cups of coffee later, they felt they'd known each other for years.

Anne sobbed when admitting she hadn't been to visit her son, saying that it was so far away and her daughter, Eva, had convinced her that it would be futile. She'd lost everything that year: her son, her partner, her home, her dignity. Moving to Georgia, where nobody knew them, was a new life. She'd even changed their surname to Bray. B for Brown, and Ray from Jonah.

She told Trudi every single thing about her life and the parentage of her two children. She beamed with pride when extolling tales of Trevor as a youngster. How different Eva was in comparison!

"But he was the pastor, you see, Trudi. We young girls knew no better. We were led to think we were chosen. He said it was *God's* will, *His* divine intervention. My mother didn't believe me, of course. She called me the most awful names but when a baby arrives, who could not believe it was right after all? Fortunately, Trevor didn't inherit his father's demented genes. Or did he? See, that's what I don't want to admit, that my son developed into his father. If a man of God rapes a young woman, does it automatically follow that his spawn will turn out to be the same?"

"Mrs, Bray, I don't believe that, no. It's that unanswered, debatable question about nature or nurture, isn't it? In my line of work, I see so many lost souls. They're not all bad people, just down on their luck, but they will be ultimately classed as bad people because of their unfortunate circumstances. I don't see your son as a bad person, and clearly you don't either."

Anne couldn't hold back her tears any longer, "I've never considered Trevor capable of doing anything but good. Wild, imaginative, crazy, but never cruel, ever."

Trudi grinned. This was music to her ears. It was such a relief to hear his mother's version. She dared to go further…

"I've told you that we've got a nice friendship thing going, I've been to visit him a couple of times now. We write to each other often and I can tell you his letters are fabulous. He makes me laugh out loud. He tells me about the conversations he has with the guy in the cell next to him. They discuss everything from religion to extraterrestrials, dinosaurs to life in Heaven.”

“Trevor was like that,” Anne grinned, “talked non-stop about everything he was interested in. He felt he knew everything there was to know, too.”

Trudi chuckled. “He says he’s 100 percent innocent, Mrs. Bray.” She was nervous now; she was about to lay all her cards on the table. “He told me he loved Alice and he would never do anything to hurt her. Likewise, Jonah, the man he looked up to, who taught him everything about beekeeping and did so much for your family. He admired his many talents, his photography and the fact that he incorporated both hobbies into one, he told me – ”

Anne interrupted her, “He did all of that, God rest his soul. He treated both my children as if they were his own. Jonah and I were school pals, too. Our parents also had known each other. Oh Lordy, the dirt we sweep under the carpets. It’s so unbelievable I can’t think about it, but Trevor was correct about Jonah’s photography skills, I’ve still got his camera. I found it a couple of days after the incident.”

Anne continued, “I went over there, you know, to try to make some sense of it all. It saddened me to see all his beautiful beehives destroyed and one or two bees flying around as if in mourning. Can't even fathom how to use the thing. It's just something I have left of him."

Trudi was almost hyperventilating. "Jonah's camera? You have it? Could I possibly have a look?"

"I think it needs to be charged or something because I can't even get it to switch on."

Exactly as Anne had said, the battery was completely dead.

"If you had your life to live over again, Cole, would you? You know, would you do anything differently?"

"Is that another of your god-damned stupid hypothetical questions, kid?" Cole was practically drooping his shoulders at yet another soul-searching question that he had no positive answer to. How could he?

"You asking me about hindsight again? Doesn't every single person in the universe wonder the same damned thing? I'm sure this fine hotel would be empty if we all had the opportunity to turn the clocks back. You do come out with some rubbish statements at times. I throw back your question to you, Nipper. Would you?"

Trevor contemplated for a second. "I don't see how I could. I just don't see how I could have done anything differently - apart from maybe not getting involved with a girl. Not that I regret that. She was perfect."

"Seems to me she was probably the wrong girl then. If there was ever such a thing."

"Was your girl the wrong girl?"

"Like I told you, 'there is no such thing'."

"For once, Cole, I agree with you. I think these prisons hold more wrong men than wrong women."

"Ditto, 8356, for once *I* agree with *you*."

The two were silent for a second or two, mulling over the 'what ifs'.

"Life's like that film, 'Sliding Doors' isn't it? Wondering how our lives would be if we happened to be in a different place at a different time. And that song, 'If I could turn back time' by that Cher. I mean, all the years you've been here just waiting to die when you could've been living your best life outside if – "

"Mary, Mother of God, don't you ever shut the fuck up, boy? *If* the Virgin Mary had given birth to a girl instead of a boy, the whole damn Bible would take on a different meaning! The past cannot be changed no matter how hard you wish or pray. If Louis Armstrong hadn't landed on the moon, you wouldn't have bored everyone stupid with your crazy notions about becoming an astronaut or believing in all that bullshit about the planets and star signs. Everything happens because it just does and that's life. I hate to be the bearer of bad news but despite popular opinion, there is no ulterior Master Plan."

"He didn't!" Trevor was indignant.

"He didn't what? What you talking about?"

"It was *NEIL* Armstrong! Everybody knows that."

Cole was about to burst a blood vessel with frustration. He started to raise his voice, shouting and screaming obscenities, demanding to be moved to another cell. He'd come to the end of his tether, listening to the constant inane banter from his neighbour. If he could have punched through his cell walls again, he would have. He wanted to silence the fool for ever. He envisioned confronting him and putting his hands around the throat of the younger prisoner, watching his eyes protrude as he gasped for breath. It would be immensely satisfying.

He zoned out from any further conversation and lay back on his bed, sweating and letting memories swim over in his mind, reliving the first time he'd physically strangled his victim. It felt powerful, orgasmic. He'd watched the life drain out of her until the taunting stopped.

She was hitch-hiking alone, a guitar and rucksack swung on her back. They chatted about their music preferences; he showed her the Gibson guitar he'd stolen and said he was on his way to a music festival. She told him she was going to the same one. She had braided dreadlocks that fell down her back. Her cut-off Jeans accentuated her beautiful legs and Cole couldn't take his lustful eyes off her.

Night was approaching and Cole suggested they park for the night, ready for an early start in the morning. He cooked some burgers on an open fire and they played their guitars together, laughing and singing. She admired the songs he'd written, the flattery he took as an invitation for payment for the ride.

She wasn't unwilling to 'pay' for the ride and food either; lots of female hitch-hikers realised that sex was an expected remunerative settlement. A condom was a cheaper ticket than an electronic other.

She shouldn't have laughed at his pathetic, selfish, sexual performance. The others didn't: they had been more afraid; but this woman, this bitch, wasn't as naive as his previous, younger, conquests. She was used to bigger, better, and more proficient.

His previous kills paled into significance after he killed his hitch-hiking companion. This was the *real* thrill; actually performing the ritual with his own bare hands.

He opened a can of beer and drank the whole lot without stopping. He belched loudly then – laughing – urinated on her lifeless body. He took out a penknife and sliced off a dreadlock, tucking it inside his Gibson guitar. He would remember this moment every time he strummed the strings to his music.

31: Trudi

Trudi was mega-surprised that Anne had allowed her to take Jonah's camera away, knowing its sentimental value, even though she'd adamantly declared to return on Monday morning after Eva was back in school.

She had no compatible chargers for the camera, so decided to walk into town to find somewhere that would sell one. Pawn shops were full of hundreds of obsolete wires, chargers, etc. Ten minutes later, something plugged in and connected to electricity enabled the camera to flicker and Trudi held her breath.

"We have lift off" she giggled to the uninterested broker behind the counter.

"Two dollars and fifty cents," he mumbled, not taking his eyes off his computer screen depicting two females in a compromising position.

She left him a five dollar bill and hurried back to her rented room where she proceeded to watch everything from Jonah's camera on her TV screen.

Oh… My,,, God!!!!!!!!!

Dearest Trevor,

Pray tell me who is your bestest friend in the whole wide world? The answer, obviously, is Moi! I'm coming over imminently, I've requested an urgent visitation. Later, amigo. Xx

Dear Trudi,

Don't come, please. I'm not in the mood for a visit. Have just heard that Cole's execution has been brought forward, which saddens me because it's now all so real. Even though I despise the man, I don't wish him dead. I've developed a sort of friendship with him which I'm sure you will have difficulty in understanding, but what is that saying "to walk in another man's shoes?"

She was quickly on to the phone to her friend. "Elaine, get me a visit to Trevor, please. Like, pronto. Now, immediately."

"Why the urgency? Why don't you go through the proper channels like always?"

"Hello? Because I need to go now, today, tomorrow. Pleeeeease."

*   *   *   *   *

"Trevor. I'm gonna waste no time because we both know we've only minutes. I've come a long way, yet again, to see you. Don't even dare to interrupt me because, honey, I have a lot to say, and our clock is ticking. I *KNOW* you are innocent because I have the proof!"

Trevor looked at her as though she'd lost all her marbles.

"His camera!" she squealed. "Your mother gave me Jonah's camera and it's all on there, everything. Your mom had no idea because she couldn't charge the battery and – "

"You saw my mom? Trudi, you saw my mom? How is she?"

"I did, Trevor, I decided to pay her a visit. I told you I would try to find her and I did. I also found the absolute truth to prove your innocence! I've given the whole lot to Matt, after taking a copy, of course, which I have kept totally separate. Trevor - you, my friend, are going to get your retribution. You *will* be declared a free man."

"I don't understand what you're saying. What about Jonah's camera? How did my mother get it?"

"Who cares how she got it? The fact is that she had it, and… Oh, my God, Trevor, it's pretty graphic to say the least! Yeah, sorry, I had to witness you and Alice losing your virginity to each other, and may I say, honey, you were sweet."

She was almost in tears as she continued, "See, Jonah was caring and protective. Perhaps a little too much and I don't know whether he intended to watch you and record it or if he just stumbled upon the pair of you? You knew the guy more than most, so I'll leave it to you to decide. Anyway, these photos are your saving grace, Sunshine, because, as you rightly declared, you left Alice after kissing her goodbye. However… Jonah must have been there, and then the mob appeared."

Pausing long enough to catch her breath, Trudi rambled on. "He took some pics of an altercation with Alice and her older brother. Seems the brother was angry at what he'd witnessed; angry or aroused - possibly both. He then strangled Alice, and as she fell

238

to the ground under his brutality. He then proceeded to rape her. Poor Jonah witnessed the whole thing. God knows why he didn't intervene. But he captured it, Trevor, it proves your innocence."

"That's absolute bullshit, Trudi. Jonah would never have spied on me, and that's what you're insinuating."

She smiled at him, "I don't have to insinuate anything. Matt Hansome is coming to see you tomorrow. He can explain everything. He'll be bringing your mother, too."

Trevor felt numb. Trudi's words reverberated in his subconscious as he tried to focus on the scene after leaving his young lover. Her own brother raped her after he'd made love with her. And Jonah? Watched and took photographs? That wasn't possible. And his mother was finally coming to visit him. How should he act? He wanted to cry, thinking of the numbers of innocents past, present, and future.

"I daren't think. I can't equate what you're saying. Why would Rocky kill his own flesh and blood? He was my friend, too. No, Trudi, it's completely untrue. All the brothers adored their sister, they would never have done anything to hurt her. You're wrong."

"Matthew will explain everything. I'm paying him, by the way, so don't worry about your mother having to fork out any more. Keep writing in that notebook of yours. Oh, and by the way, sorry I forgot to ask you earlier, but you said your friend's execution date has been brought forward. I don't know what to say to you."

"He's hardly a *friend* in the loving term of endearment. He's a 'cellie', someone we call another close inmate. Close in proximity, not in feelings, although we have kinda become close, I suppose. We've talked a lot, you see. It's all becoming too real to accept. I'm scared Trudi. I've been living on a knife edge ever since that day. I don't want to die. I don't want to be like Cole and having only so many hours to tick off, afraid to go to sleep because of wasting valuable hours of living. He says he's okay with it, it's what he's been hoping for, but I don't believe him."

Trevor stopped talking for a moment, gazing around his small cubicle. "The executioners are different just lately. It's as though they're anticipating all their Christmases coming soon. They're laughing and joking with us, no doubt luring us into a false sense of security. They're feeding on our fears in their mock friendship, they will know our fate before we do. Even though I'm sure Cole deserves what's in store for him, it saddens me because too many people I've had as friends have died, or I've lost. Hmmm. It's weird."

"What's weird?"

"The story you've just told me. I can't get my head around you describing Jonah clicking away with his camera instead of rushing to help Alice. He could not have done that, Trudi. Besides, it wasn't in his nature to stand by and do nothing to help. He hated injustice."

"Well, somebody took those pictures, my friend, and with his camera."

Trevor's head bobbed up and down in concentration, trying to re-picture the scene. "Hindsight, hey? If only I hadn't been worried about getting back to close Eva's window and insisted on walking Alice home. I wouldn't be sitting here now, would I? And the miserable cow let me down, too, cos she had locked her damned window by the time I got back but fortunately she'd left the front door open."

"Really?" Trudi enquired. "Did she often do things to piss you off?" she chuckled.

"All the time! She's a cunning little so-and-so, more often than not." He shook his head in despair. "She's my baby sister but hey, we're not alike at all. Eva's very aloof, withdrawn, secretive. Me? I wear my heart on my sleeve. Jonah tried his hardest with her and Mom but she wouldn't budge."

"Wouldn't budge? How?"

"Why do you wanna know about Eva?"

"No reason. I just wondered why she never wrote to you."

"I don't know. She's real smart, though. Top in her class at everything, but she never had any friends as such. A bit of a loner, an introvert. She'd cause a scene about going to church every Sunday and hated animals which I could never understand because I love them all. She'd tease me about my bees, said I was boring because I spent so many hours with them. She didn't like me having a girlfriend either, said it was 'unnatural'"

"Unnatural? Haha, ah bless her. She was perhaps a tad jealous of you because you were growing up, doing what is 'natural'?"

"It's not natural to stick a straw up the ass of a frog and blow it up, though, is it, and then squeal with laughter when it explodes?"

Trudi stopped laughing, "No, that doesn't sound like the kind of thing a sweet little girl would do. I certainly didn't do anything like that. Anyway, we're moving away from the important stuff. Your lawyer and your mother will be here to explain more to you. Matt is busy busy, busy working all hours God sends on this new evidence. You can't possibly be kept here once the governor sees what's on the camera."

"I hardly dare to believe, Trudi."

"Then start to dare."

32: Matt Hansome

Matt had studied the photographs on Jonah's camera. It was a Canon, digital, so every image was dated, leaving no doubt that his client was as innocent as he'd proclaimed. But what Matt struggled to understand was why the pictures were taken, and if indeed it had been Jonah behind the lens. Why on earth did he not intervene when obviously a young girl was being raped and murdered? What sick, demented individual would witness and record such a heinous crime without rushing to her aid?

Was Jonah some dreadful pervert who got off on something like this, then went back home to study his artwork and prolong his enjoyment? It didn't sound like the profile of the man he understood him to be. But it *was* Jonah's camera, the receipt was tucked inside the empty case found in his home.

It was evident he had a passion for photography, his home was full of his creativity, his framed bee photographs, with others, were displayed on every wall.

He made a copy of all the photographs, starting with the young lovers hugging. The time showed it was 12:10 a.m. Alice's serene smiling face was looking up at Trevor's, bathed by the glow of the moon. There were many others that followed, and Matt felt an encompassing amount of guilt at witnessing these two young people clumsily declare their feelings for each other.

After Trevor's departure, the photographic evidence took on a more sinister stance. Rocky, the older brother, confronting his sister, his hands around her throat with hers seemingly trying to remove them, her legs buckling under his force.

Another of Rocky with his jeans round his ankles, raping his precious and adored sister who appeared motionless.

Rocky again, tucking his shirt in his jeans, glaring daggers at the photographer. Was this when he realised he'd been captured and realised he had to kill the man photographing everything, knowing he could spend a lifetime behind bars?

Anne had eventually confessed to Trudi that she discovered the camera in Eva's bedroom. How did Eva come to be in possession of Jonah's camera? And if she *knew* what was on there, why did she not say anything to support her brother's innocence? Nothing added up.

Matt needed to visit Alice's mother. He'd read and reread all the brothers' statements but acknowledged he must be missing something. If the mother refused his request, it didn't matter: he'd go down the legal route and obtain a subpoena.

"You've certainly got Matt working hard for his crust again, Trudi; and me, for that matter. It's like *deja vu*. Alice's mother was adamant she wasn't going to be interviewed again, which we both expected, to be honest. Can't blame the woman can you? Dredging it all up again, her poor daughter."

"I don't blame her at all, it must be horrendous to have it dissected again after all this time, but it's necessary taking into consideration a young man's life is at stake. And as a mother, she understands that and ultimately wants to know who's responsible for the murder of her daughter."

"But those photos, Trudi. Those of the older brother. How can any mother cope with *that* knowledge?"

Trudi nodded, "I know, I know... I really don't know! God, how is she going to cope? But the camera never lies, so they say, and she's going to be mortified. So was Trevor's mother, by the way."

Elaine topped up her friend's glass of wine, perfunctorily. "Here's to mothers everywhere," she hiccuped, "and here's to freedom of choice on abortions for those who choose not to be mothers."

Trudi raised her glass, laughing in agreement, "And to us, should we ever be lucky enough to find someone suitable to want to make us mothers."

"I'm getting a dog," Elaine announced out of the blue, her wineglass hovering precariously mid-air, "a Beagle, from the rescue centre. So much easier than having a baby. No morning sickness, no labour or stretch-marks, no compulsory 'school parent days', just a daily walk in the park, food in the bowl, a ball to play with and 'bob's your uncle', all for the minimal fee of forty dollars. She's been spayed and chipped and her name is Betty. Like Betty Boop, do you remember?"

Trudi looked at her friend as if not quite believing. "Are you being serious? A dog? You're out at work every day. Honey, that's not really fair to the dog, is it?"

"Yes, it is," she answered back assertively, "I'm re-homing, adopting. Giving a lost cause a second chance to live. Very similar to what you've been doing for Trevor if you think about it. I might not be available for her 24/7, but who can be? Anyway, she's coming home tomorrow. Just wait till I show you her pink blanket."

"We have two weeks until it takes place. The Governor will be in attendance but not his wife; she's declined. Fox News will cover the whole thing, along with several media outlets, obviously only from the outside. Cave has given me a sealed letter to give to Trevor Brown on the day of his release, if this goes ahead, of course. He has also informed me that he wishes to recite his final words in front of an audience, I've yet to clarify his full intention. It could be an apology to his victims' families or something else and that's why I haven't agreed to this request as yet."

"Do any of you gentlemen have anything you need to add? Pinkstone, have the caterers been informed of his last meal requirements?"

Pinkstone cleared his throat, "Not exactly, sir."

"What do you mean 'not exactly?', you know full well they can have anything they ask for."

Pinkstone shoved a piece of paper towards Statham. "Here's his list, Warden. Do you think the caterers can fulfil his dietary requisitions?"

Statham read the words out loud:

"A magnum of Bollinger for breakfast, to wash down six kippers with scrambled eggs. For lunch (I'm assuming I'm getting lunch too?) I would like a steak pie with mashed potatoes, corn, gravy, and my mother's homemade cornbread. Just like Bud Rogers requested, if you remember.

I need to depart this world full to the brim so that I am carried to where I'm going to be murdered. Yes, that's right, murdered! You see the irony? We are alike after all.

I'm praying I have the opportunity to partake of dinner, too, to finish off the festivities, so to speak, in which case I'd like chicken breasts. Caroline's. She was a chick and had very small but desirable breasts, but tell the chef not to add any garlic. She's more of a 'sweet and sour' type. A joint would be most welcome, too. A decent one, real stuff. A big joint with a bottle of whisky from Islay - no accoutrements to water it down, either. There's a fabulous purveyor I came across in Ohio that specialise in quality liquor and he had a couple of bottles of vintage Lagavulin at the time I paid a visit. I couldn't afford to buy one and too many cameras to risk helping myself, so I left a twenty dollar bill deposit and told him to save it for me. I promised the man I would return one day to pay the outstanding amount."

The warden lowered the letter and looked at his men. "His mother's home-made cornbread? The cocky son of a bitch. He's a card and a half if ever such a thing existed. Here," he threw the paper away, "let the cooks decide. And tell them to omit the obligatory sedatives. I will relish watching the monster tremble."

"But sir – " Pinkstone tried.

"That's all, gentlemen. We're done here."

35: Hazel and Matthew

Hazel – Alice's mother - was understandably very reluctant to receive Matt. Her 'mother-hen' protectiveness trait was unquestionable. She had the boys, all of them, to comfort whilst still mourning her daughter privately. The last thing she needed now, after all this time, was for the whole resurrection of that indescribably painful night.

As she opened the front door, Matt felt the force of her dismissal of anything he was about to reveal or ask. She portrayed an aura of confrontation before anything had been said. "My boys are out. All of them. What do you need?"

"My name is Matthew Hansome and, as I'm sure you are aware, I represent Trevor Carlton Brown, the young man accused of the rape and murder of your daughter, Alice. Please believe me when I say I am truly sorry to come to you today to have to ask you some very painful questions, but – "

"Don't stand on my threshold blubbering apologies. Come inside quickly! I don't need to give the neighbours any more ammunition to taunt us with. Come!"

Matt entered Hazel's home, amazed to encounter what appeared to be a shrine dedicated to her one and only daughter. It was surreal as every wall was covered floor to ceiling in pictures of Alice, from a baby to a beautiful teenager. He knew people mourned the loss of their loved ones but had never experienced anything on this magnitude.

"Miles is at music school for the blind. He's learning to be a saxophonist. The twins, Oscar and Otis, are at their school, and Rocky is at work. He has a full time job now, working at the slaughterhouse. Ask your questions quickly, because once the boys get home, that's it. I have to feed them." She sat in front of him, almost accusatory, wringing her hands rhythmically, nervously.

Matt was good with words, always had been. "You're a good woman, Hazel, raising your boys in the way that they had that sibling closeness, that special bond. They looked out for each other, didn't they?"

Hazel beamed proudly as Matt continued, "Yes, you did a fine job as a mother. Much like Trevor's mother." He dared to glance across to her for a reaction. "You had the same mother-and-daughter closeness that Anne had with her son, which is rather precious, isn't it?"

"It is," she spat angrily, "but that has nothing to do with the fact that he murdered my beautiful daughter and then continued on his rampage to kill his mother's partner. I trusted that boy, sir. I gave my daughter my blessing for their union. Now I'm left to pick up the pieces and have to try to live a normal life. It's not possible. I have to teach her siblings to be more cautious in their choice of friends. Alice and Trevor had known each other since their early school days. He was family, as far as I was concerned. Tell me, Mr Hansome, do you have children?"

Matt faltered slightly, "We don't, not yet anyway, but we're trying hard. I think parenting must be immensely challenging and I'm not sure I'm up to that particular challenge yet. I think one must worry every day, asking if you re doing right, teaching them life's lessons. I'm sure you and Trevor's mother had the same worries all parents have. I remember my mother saying 'as babies they break your arms, when they're older they break your heart'. Would you agree with that, too?"

"I'm certain Anne Brown can agree with that. Her son broke many hearts. I watch the television, Mr Hansome, I've seen that everybody is expecting that boy to get off, it's disgusting I tell you, disgusting! What sorcery is in place for the decision to change after all this time? His DNA sealed his guilt. What's with this 'new evidence' they're yelling about? Where's the justice for my poor Alice?"

Matt felt dreadful, knowing he was going to add further misery to one mother after unburdening it from the other. "I have the most unpleasant task of leaving this with you. The Chief of Police will return here later this evening to ask your elder son to accompany him to the station for questioning. I'm very sorry," he said, handing over the envelope containing a photograph of Rocky arguing with his sister. Just the one to prove her daughter was still alive after Trevor's departure.

He stood to leave, hating to see the confusion on the woman's face, "You should get him a lawyer, as soon as you can. Goodbye."

It was a small interview room; the same one he'd sat in before when he and his brother gave their statements. He was nervous, angry, and stunk of death.

Very few people have the capability to kill. Or should that be very few people have a conscience when they kill? The slaughterhouse had a constant flow of butchers pass through their gates, each strutting bravado of their employment. Most who applied for the job couldn't hack it after a couple of days. The pitiful cries of the animals as they were slaughtered was too much for any normal person to bear. They knew what was happening, and that's why the floor was covered in animal shit, then blood - lots and lots of it.

The slaughterhouse was located miles away in a secluded field that represented nothing of the horrors behind the huge metal warehouse. Cows grazed solemnly outside, aware of their numbers diminishing hourly. If one was to drive by this field, a palpable eerie sadness hung in the air.

Not for Rocky, though, it provided him a good income. It put clothes on his family's backs and food in their stomachs. It was just that: employment. Emotions were irrelevant.

He remembered his first kill, or rather his first paid kill. It was a calf, and he had watched as it was dragged away from its screaming mother. His predecessor had shown him several times the correct way to administer the knife to cause the least pain and distress. "Does it really matter?" he asked his colleague, it's gonna die so once it's dead, it's dead."

"It *does* matter, you need to be quick, very quick. The animals outside will hear everything and we try to avoid any unnecessary suffering. Once you've got them on the hoist, the throat slitting must be instantaneous. Then they'll be wheeled along on the pulley to the butchers whilst the blood drains. The sheep are the worst, they look into your eyes and – "

"Hence the expression 'like lambs to the slaughter'? Aw, don't worry, I've had my fair share of rabbits and deer to kill. Always considered it free food."

His tutor grimaced: there was nothing 'free' or liberating about killing.

The out-of-sight cameras began filming as the interviewers explained the reasons for him being sequestered. Rocky had already rehearsed his excuse for the photograph his mother had shown him, totally unprepared to see dozens more spread out in front, now frantically debating what his answers were going to be.

He sweated, remembering every detail of the photographs taunting him, realising his lies were going to be futile. Defeat inevitable.

"I want a lawyer," was all he said.

Hazel sat in the waiting room, twisting a handkerchief in her wet palms, worrying about her other sons who had seemed exceptionally quiet when she had explained everything to them, over dinner.

He lay in his holding cell that night, arms at the back of his head, his ankles crossed, eyes wide open as his mind relived the memories again.

He had known his sister's rendezvous time, and what was going to happen, and it had sickened him. His sweet, beautiful sister was about to be defiled by a stupid black boy when she deserved so much better.

He'd overheard her conversations with their mother and watched her collect the contraceptive pill from the pharmacy. He had this feeling that festered in the pit of his stomach. Her constant smile ate away at him, poisoning his once brotherly love. He also knew that someone else shared his disapproval of the forthcoming liaison: Eva - Trevor's own sister.

Eva had matured physically and mentally far quicker than Trevor. She was also very different to him. She'd had a secret crush on Rocky from as far back as she could remember, always trying to seek out his approval, his company, which would annoy him immensely as a kid, and her for his refusal to acknowledge that fact. She was adamant she was going to do everything she could to garner his friendship, no matter what.

"It's going to be soon," she'd told him. "The contraceptive pill has to be in her system long enough so she doesn't get pregnant. Heaven forbid *that* happens! I'll keep you informed. I'm sure you'll be able to find a way to thank me."

He knew she liked him, she'd made it abundantly obvious to the point of being embarrassing, but at the end of the day black and white didn't mix, in his jurisdiction. It was a line that just wasn't to be crossed.

'If you can't see, feel, or hear colours, then how can you say it's wrong, Rock? I don't understand because my world is different from yours. I don't judge like you do. I judge on sounds and feelings. It's so simple. You should try closing your eyes again, like Mom made us do. Do you remember that? She tried to make you all understand what it's like for me. Trevor's nice, why don't you like his skin? Is it really that horrible because I didn't think it felt any different from mine.'

Those words again from Miles, his blind brother. His 'all seeing' blind brother. Oscar and Otis were too young to understand. And Alice, his stupid, stupid, beautiful sister must have been blind, too.

The interview reconvened at 9:30 a.m. the next morning. The two previous interviewers appeared fresh and eager to continue the interrogation.

"You strangled your sister then raped her. Here..." she said, shoving the photograph towards him. "Is that an act of brotherly love?"

Rocky said nothing.

"Who were you surprised to see here?" She showed him the picture of his angered face, towards the camera.

He still declined to answer.

"Jonah's camera was found in Trevor Brown's sister's possession. How do you think it ended up there? Was she trying to save you by incriminating her own brother? Did you promise her something to make it all worthwhile? We know she had a big crush on you. It's pretty much general knowledge."

All the words spilling out were choking him. He felt doomed. What was his mother going to think? He couldn't answer, the truth pounding in his ears.

"Are you gay, Rocky?"

He jerked upright from his seat, his answer stuck in his throat.

"It's just that you couldn't have ejaculated when you raped your sister. Only Trevor's DNA was found. Did that piss you off, to realise your friend was more of a man than you? Did you think it would make you more of a man to rape someone?"

"And 'Rocky' isn't your *real* name is it? You adapted that from someone you admired, that infamous, unforgettable character who inspired young men the world over. Isn't it true your Christian name is Shirley? I can imagine it must have been pretty rough growing up with a name that has female connotations, especially considering your surname."

Rocky shrank visibly upon hearing the dreaded name his mother had christened him. Shirley! What had possessed her? How did they know that?

"And your sexual act on your sister was revenge, wasn't it? You wanted to get back at Trevor because he was the one you really wanted. He had always been the one. You wanted to shift the blame on skin colour, pretending to be the oh-so-caring brother, but that wasn't so at all. And then you used the affections of his sister, Eva, to assist you in your dual scheming knowing she would do anything to win your favour."

"Did she know? Eva? Did she know it was her brother you wanted rather than her? OK. You don't have to answer that right now, but tell us how you managed to convince her to collude in your scheme?"

"I need the bathroom," Rocky said softly, ashamedly.

Later, Rocky's lawyer sat aside him.

"You do realise that your life long school friend, the man you wanted as a sexual partner, has been sitting in death row, accused of a crime committed by you? Is that why you took the job of a slaughterer, to release your pent-up frustration? To inflict pain on other innocent beings in an endeavour to release your own?"

Rocky looked to his lawyer for guidance, who shrugged his shoulders, "up to you."

"It's a job. That's all."

"It's a job," she repeated, smiling, knowing her next statement would irritate him, "and we all have jobs to do. Mine is to establish the truth, sift out the chaff from the grain and determine what is worth keeping. *Surely* you understand?"

Rocky cringed, knowing full well the 'surely' comment was a dig at his name, the way she emphasised it, slowly, purposefully.

"I'm *not* gay" he said, forcefully, "you've got that all wrong. I loved my sister, of course I did, but not like that, it wasn't like that."

"Then why don't you tell us what it was like?"

Rocky reluctantly glanced at all the photographs spread out in front of him and knew he had lost. He stared at the brutalised lifeless body of his sweet, beautiful sister, wondering what had possessed him to commit such a revolting act, wishing he had never been there and worried about the effect his unimaginable behaviour was going to have on his mother and brothers after all they'd endured. He couldn't answer the question because he couldn't find the words, none that would ever adequately explain anything anyway. His throat hurt from the pain of trying to stifle his tears.

"And why did you then go and kill Jonah? Was it to silence him?"

"I didn't kill Jonah. I didn't see him. It wasn't he who took these photographs."

The interviewers looked at each other in confusion. "What? But... if it wasn't Jonah... who was it?"

37: Alice's Mother

It was the worst nightmare a mother could ever contemplate. Her teenage daughter wasn't home. Her boys were in their rooms, unusually nonchalant, apart from Miles, who appeared to be totally perplexed.

She'd had a good night with her friend. They'd reminisced, as they usually did, over a bottle of inexpensive white wine on their reunions.

The twins, Otis and Otto, were fast asleep in their bunk beds. Rocky was cross-legged on the floor, playing a computer game. Miles was in the living room, on the settee, rocking backwards and forwards, scratching relentlessly at his wrists.

She sat beside him, "Hey, Honey, I'm home," she chuckled as she touched his hand, "did you all have a good night tonight? Is your sister not back yet?"

She knew her daughter well enough to know she was meeting up night after night with her long-time friend, Trevor; and she was pleased, knowing that he was a decent young man. She also knew that her daughter was mature enough to take preventative measures for any unwanted pregnancy as they'd discussed this, and Hazel had taken her to the clinic to get the contraceptive pill.

Alice had confided her feelings to her mother that she and Trevor were going to cement their lifelong relationship the week after her eighteenth birthday.

Hazel could have never imagined a night so indifferent to any other until she heard a forceful knocking on her back door. She excused herself from Miles, wondering who could be calling so late.

"Don't answer the door, Mom," Miles pleaded, "please don't."

38: Duke

They called him The Duke, Trevor's new cellmate. They had nicknamed him The Duke because his surname was Prince. Hardly royalty, Trevor pondered, although he did look somehow regal, with his blond hair and bright blue eyes, and a huge tattoo of a crown of thorns around his bicep.

Trevor had never understood the fascination with tattoos and body piercing. They were an ugly and obviously painful mutilation of one's skin. He wondered why anyone would want to inflict unnecessary pain in that way and be left for evermore with a reminder of a youthful act of stupidity. He remembered when his sister decided to pierce her ears and he cringed when he realised she was going to do it herself! She didn't bat an eyelid. She'd taken a safety pin from her mother's sewing kit and an ice cube from the ice box. She'd held the ice cube on her ear lobe for a few seconds then shoved the safety pin all the way through. It looked horrendous, Trevor told her, but Eva had said the safety pin was only temporary. She was going to ask Jonah to buy her a nice pair of diamond studs, and perhaps a nose ring to match. She had no reason to doubt he would.

Seeing The Duke's tattoo reminded him of that afternoon. Eva was possibly twelve or thirteen, he couldn't remember exactly, but he could recall his feeling of horror and repulsion as he witnessed her doing that, and her smile spread as she assessed herself in the mirror afterwards.

He remembered telling her that their mother would go bonkers because she was too young to be doing such a stupid thing. She just laughed, dismissively, stating 'it was her body, her decision'. He had no doubt she would have more piercings of some description, now.

"So, what's the Caveman like? Is he as cool as they say he is?" The Duke asked Trevor.

"Depends on what you've heard them say about him, I guess."

"Well, you're the only one he's talked to for the last how many years. After that other guy, what was his name again? Rogers. Buck Rogers? No, *Bud* Rogers… That's it! I remember that guy. He'd been in 'the club' for decades. An old man when they finally decided to fry him."

"He was 62. That's not old."

"It was for him, spent all his life here. Never seeing sunshine or feeling its rays on his skin. Never feeling human companionship, or love. Did you know -- "

"And do you not ask yourself the question why he didn't have those simple luxuries? Didn't he forfeit all those rights before he was condemned?"

Duke looked at him with contempt, unable to comprehend his lack of understanding, being a fellow inmate.

"Pardon me. I forgot who I was talking to. The squeaky-clean black boy who claims he's whiter than white. Innocent beyond doubt yet here he sits with a self-confessed murderer, no less. If I had a knife, I would cut your vicious tongue out right now, you fucking son of a bitch! Don't put yourself on a pedestal too high unless you have wings because there has never been smoke without fire as far as we're all concerned. I suggest you keep that big mouth of yours shut from now on because none of us like that more-holier-than-thou attitude. What's wrong with you? Whose side are you on, for crying out loud, and choose your allegiance wisely!"

Trevor had never been one to back down, to eat humble pie, or shut up when told to, feeling he had to say his piece. He'd often attributed this fact to his grandmother who never failed to add her quota to a conversation no matter its relevance or acceptance, he just had to leap in!

It had driven Cole completely bonkers in the past, yet now, somehow, he missed their banter. It had evoked emotions, feelings to pursue conversations even though he was averse to revealing too much information. Now he was left in total silence, albeit some mumblings from afar that he had no inclination of responding to. Truth be told, he missed *him*, that pain in the proverbial ass, that irritating number - 8356.

They'd all been dehumanised to mere numbers, which was logical considering everything was that way, dating back decades ago when everyone was given a Social Security Number; your name was no longer significant. Likewise, in prisons the world over, you would be referred to as a number. Counted less than the letters on a birth certificate. He could have debated this with Brown, as they did often over many topics. He would have taken great pleasure in educating him about the science of mathematics, the history of Archimedes and Pythagoras, then realised his stupidity at his assumption the kid wouldn't already know! But what a great topic of discussion that would have been.

Cole excelled in both numbers and words. He knew many that would only be adept in one, like his mother who had been dyslexic; excellent with numbers but struggled with words. Not so with Cole. It had been beneficial, too, when planning his next move. He'd work out the mileage, the cost of fuel per mile, how long it would take to get from A to B and ascertain how much it would cost. He'd travel mainly at night when the temperature was cooler, the roads less busy, thus avoiding hold-ups. His aliases usually contained the same amount of letters, he'd take casual employment wherever he could and be remunerated in cash; sometimes playing his guitar for small audiences in smoky bars. He didn't want to leave an electronic trail. He shopped only for essentials, surviving more often than not on roadkill and stealing from his victims, considering the Lord was providing for him.

He thought back to the question Brown asked him once, something on the lines of would he do anything different if he had his life to live over again and of course his answer would have been no, because he'd never looked back! His only regret was being careless enough to be caught.

Trevor wanted to put The Duke in the picture. "I wasn't trying to be disrespectful but there are some people who are just born rotten and deserve to be punished for the crimes they commit on the innocents. I agree with you that no man should be kept on tenterhooks for years and years wondering about their fate. That's inhumane. But likewise, sometimes delaying an execution can be a good thing because it's been proven – in some cases – that they're innocent. My case is a perfect example. If my execution had been carried out immediately, I would be dead now and the real murderer still out there living a carefree life."

Trevor continued, "I don't know about Bud Rogers' case, not all of it anyway, nor do I know any more than you about Cole, other than what I've learned since moving out of 'the club'. He's kind of a closed book about himself, apart from sometimes."

"Sometimes? What's that supposed to mean?"

Trevor smiled, reflecting on their hundreds of debates; some heated, some meaningful, others downright ludicrous.

"He would only reveal what he wanted me to know. He once told me he'd been in love and that that was his downfall, but I don't think he was capable of such an emotion. He's a very intelligent man, writes lyrics, plays the guitar, and let's face it, he must be a genius to have avoided capture for so long. He was educated, and has a deep, cultured, voice. He's the kind of man you feel you *know*, but I doubt anyone really knew him. Obviously not his family."

The Duke sat listening, attentively, admiringly. The Caveman had been a darned sight more elusive than himself who was arrested within a few hours of his crime. "You were lucky to have had that opportunity, to bond with him like you did. He's kinda revered by many."

Trevor didn't dare patronise that statement! 'Revered?' The man is pure evil!

"I've promised to include him in my book. He's sent me some lyrics he wants me to use. He's also written some for his execution, but he's not sent me that, yet. If you *revere* him that much, why don't you write to him? Everybody likes a bit of fan mail. You might get lucky and get a reply, then you'll have a keepsake, probably be worth a few bucks when you get outta here."

The Duke laughed, 'me, write a letter to the most prolific murderer here in the most prestigious Pennsylvania hotel, and expect a reply? You out of your mind, pal?"

Trevor dismissed his negativity. "Suit yourself. But if you don't do it, you'll never know, will you?" and sat down to write yet another letter to his friend, Trudi. "By the way," he suddenly thought to add, "you should write that letter, you having so much in common. Ask him why some get the death sentence as opposed to some scum bags - like you, who don't?"

"Dear Trudi,

I know I may have said 'thank you' so many times, but possibly not expressed my gratitude properly. You have been the light at the end of my dark and lonely tunnel. You gave me hope when I was floundering, joy when i was sad, my reason to believe in our justice system. I will be forever in your debt. Every day is another day towards my freedom and it's all down to you. You're a star, more precious than any in the galaxy, or the whole universe."

*   *   *   *   *

"Dear Trevor,

Helloooo! Are you drunk? Hey, isn't that what friendship is all about? Going the extra mile to help a buddy out? And don't forget, it hasn't been a one-sided arrangement, you've given me an outlet to my misery, too. You've made me laugh, you've made me think, and don't for one minute think your release is going to be the end of our friendship because, honey, there's your book we're gonna produce. I'm looking forward to being involved in that. In fact, I was going to keep this as a surprise, but I'm a gob-on-a-stick, and have to tell you I've already got the wheels in motion. A guy who's a friend of my parents is a publisher, I've already been in talks with him, and as your case is hot hot news, he's mega excited to work with us.

Elaine has also told me that Matt's having meetings with the governing bods regarding getting compensation for you, so what with your book royalties and a whacking compensation pay-out, you - my friend - will be a wealthy chap! Just imagine if they make a film out of it, too? Wowweee, you could be famous!"

That last word about being famous, worried Trevor. He didn't want his incarceration to define him. He wanted to be anonymous once he returned to the outside world. He'd even decided to write his book under a pseudonym to avoid being hounded and questioned by those with a macabre sense of wanting the nitty-gritty. He'd have to make that clear to Trudi.

"Your friend is quite the celebrity now, just like yourself. Ha-ha, isn't it ironic, don't ya think, that you two who were side by side facing absolution and now both of you have it! Ooh, but yours isn't quite as satisfying as his, is it? Well, that's not entirely true, because yours is satisfying in a different way and to different people. You're both getting what you wanted, and - of course – what you deserve."

Ryder continued, "I always knew that that young chap didn't belong here, in 'the club', next to the likes of you, but I have to admit there was 'something' about the pair of you. We've all said it. Me, Hammond, and Pinkstone. We'd listen to some of your conversations as we did our rounds, wondered how you managed to put up with him, his never-ending talk. We'd say to each other 'take the ruddy batteries out of that man and let's have some peace'."

Cole despised Ryder and was determined not to take the bait. "The kid needed to be heard. I had no option but to listen. There is no escape, as well you know; but I feel privileged to have had the opportunity to meet him again, to get to know him."

"To 'meet him again'? You met him before?"

Cole sighed, "Slip of the tongue. It's not going to be easy for him though, out there. He should keep a low profile, keep his big mouth shut or he will wish he was back here, living in oblivion."

"He's going to be quite a wealthy individual too, got a huge compensation coming to him, courtesy of the state. A book deal as well, I hear they're saying."

Cole was silent as Ryder continued, "Pity you won't get chance to read his book. I've heard you're getting a big mention, but you'll be old news before the first chapter's done," Ryder chuckled.

"Well, the written word lives on, doesn't it? Can't be erased or unsaid, a deed undone; something learned cannot be unlearned, a sight unseen or a sound unheard… What prevents you from sleeping soundly at nights, Ryder? Does your conscience play havoc with your dreams, or are you, too, like us here, waiting and praying for the ultimate forgiveness?"

40: Trevor and the Duke

"What will happen to The Caveman; you know, afterwards?" Trevor asked.

"How do you mean, 'afterwards'?" Duke replied.

"Him, The Caveman. What will they do with his body? Do they take him somewhere?"

"Oh! Well, yeah. Once he's actually been confirmed dead, he'll be transferred to a funeral home where his family can make arrangements for collection and either bury him or cremate him. Why? You planning on sending a floral tribute?"

"I see," said Trevor thoughtfully, dismissing his sarcasm, "but what if they don't? What if he hasn't any family left that care? Remember, he killed his parents and brother. Then what?"

"You ask a shitload of questions, don't you? I believe in that case, they're interred in the prisons' graveyard. So, he'll remain here forevermore. No peace for the wicked, hey?"

"We are lucky, aren't we, Duke? We do at least have people who care about us."

"Speak for yourself. Seems you're the only one with Lady Luck on your side. My family don't care if I rot here. I'll probably end up in the same place as your friend, Cole, and many others like us. Never really bothered with all that happy family malarkey, actually. Doesn't matter where they put your body, it's just dead meat. They can flush me down the toilet for all I care."

Trevor listened to The Duke's response, saddened at his flippancy regarding where or what would be his final resting place. "You could make some kind of will, you know. Bequeath your organs to those needing desperate transplants, then you will have absolved yourself in God's eyes, and a part of you would remain living. Have you considered that?"

The Duke was flagging, becoming exhausted with the never-ending barrage from his cell-mate. "Might decide to leave my body to medical science. Like I said, when you're dead you're dead, it doesn't matter what they do, does it? They can chop me up and distribute my bits and pieces wherever they desire, I won't give a damn. Anyway, I'm hoping not to die here, I hope to wake up dead in a bed full of beautiful naked women who shagged the last breath out of me."

Trevor did the maths. By the time The Duke was released, he'd be too old to raise a smile, let alone an erection!

41: Trevor's Release

It was Friday morning, 9:00 a.m. on the 1st of July. Anne sat apprehensively in a waiting room with Matt Hansome and Trudi. It was surreal: it felt glorious and yet she was nervous. Both girls had stayed overnight in a small motel just a couple of miles from the prison. They'd passed the time allowing themselves a little indulgence to be beautified, visiting a local hairdressing salon, treating themselves to a manicure too, in an endeavour to feel extra special when they came face-to-face with their freed man.

Anne had had to invest in a new dress due to the extra pounds she'd accumulated since hearing of her son's acquittal. She'd celebrated excessively after years of being unable to appreciate food. Her selfish euphoria was only tainted by the knowledge that Alice's own mother was losing another child. She hadn't deserved that.

Warden Statham entered the room with Elizabeth, his secretary, asking if anyone would like refreshments whilst waiting for the formalities to be finalised, apologising for the delay and explaining it could take another hour, or thereabouts.

Outside, the frenzied crowd of news crews and photographers grew, mingling with hundreds of well-wishers and anti-death campaigners. Anne, Matt, and Trudi had avoided them by taking an alternative route into the prison grounds, Anne - determined to keep her new identity private.

And then the door opened, and a suited young man stood in the entrance, looking slightly uncomfortable but bearing the biggest smile Trudi had ever seen. His teeth seemed to take up all of his face as his lips reached his ears.

All three chairs scraped loudly as they stood to welcome him, and Trevor didn't know which of his three favourite people to acknowledge first. His lawyer for his professionalism and ability to get him acquitted, his friend for her unbridled belief in him and determination to be heard, or his mother for just being her. Matt and Trudi made the decision for him and just stood still as his tearful mother walked slowly towards him, her arms opened wide.

42: Trevor's New-Found Freedom

Matt, or rather Elaine as his Personal Assistant, had rented a private villa miles and miles away from the prison facility Trevor had just been released from. It was paid for by Elaine's best friend, Trudi. It was the most perfect, isolated retreat for them all to sit back and breathe whilst they discussed and debated their next course of action.

The media was desperate for an interview with the newly released prisoner, needing to know every scrap of information they could get their grubby hands on. Trevor was in admiration of his mother for deciding on a new surname for herself and Eva, thus avoiding unscrupulous reporters coming to her door.

"Bray is a great name you chose, Mom. I'm happy you acknowledged Jonah in that way. I wish the two of you had married. He was worthy of you. Why didn't you?"

Anne raised her eyebrows, "Because the fool wouldn't ask me unless I disclosed who fathered you and Eva! And even your grandmother didn't believe me, so why would he?"

Trudi turned quickly from Trevor to Anne, in confusion, placing her hand on Trevor's reassuringly, "Does he not know who his father is then, Anne?" She hoped she wasn't overstepping the mark, because *she* knew; his mother had poured her heart out to her, told *her* everything. They sat there waiting for an answer, Matt, Trudi, Trevor.

Anne straightened her shoulders and stared her son in the face, her head did that wagging dog expression, the wobbly sort seen in the back of cars, "It was the pastor," she declared, "Franco. Franco Perkins. He's your father: Eva's, too."

Trevor glared back at her, unable to comprehend how that unholy man could be his biological father, remembering that Sunday he'd turned up at their house, demanding to be patronised, and then good old Jonah had turned up to save the day. That despicable piece of trash was his father? Well, that gave him another reason to thank the Lord he'd disappeared from their lives.

Matt, deep in thought, chimed in, "and where is this pastor, this Franco Perkins, now?"

"Hopefully reaping what he's sown. Nobody knows, he left suddenly, taking all the church funds collected over the years and leaving his many offspring behind.

"Mr. Hansome," Trevor announced, "I wish to have my name changed legally. Can you arrange this, quickly? Can I call myself Cole Bray? I understand that some of you are going to point the finger and accuse me of latching on to a notorious killer, but I can't continue living as Trevor Brown anymore, I need a new identity. Plus, I will be carrying on Cave's name, he has no one else to do this."

Matt nodded, "Yes, you can. You can call yourself whatever you like. I'll take care of it."

Anne was disappointed, and made no bones about it. "Trevor," she said looking at him, "how am I ever going to forget that you're my Trevor?"

"Exactly as you did before, mother dearest," he dared tell her. "You forgot about me all that time I sat on death row. Trudi, would you please join me outside for a chin wag? Let's talk about you instead of me."

Trudi hurriedly rose from her seat to join her friend, throwing an apologetic look to her other two colleagues.

They took their seats outside and Trevor had carried out a couple of bottles of uncorked champagne, wanting to spend time alone with the only person he felt he could trust.

"Something's telling me the new 'Mr. Cole Bray' isn't a happy chappie, when he has a million reasons to be just that. Open that damned bottle, will you, and let the vintage champagne loosen your vocal chords."

Trevor couldn't help but laugh. This woman could never say anything to offend or upset him, especially now. He was sitting in the sunshine, feeling a slight breeze as he popped the expensive bubbly, watching dollars' worth spill over before it filled their glasses.

"And that's shameful, isn't it? I should be happy, and Trudi, truly I am."

They both shrieked again with laughter, "OK, stop it now. Don't keep repeating my name."

Trevor handed her a glass and raised it to clink with hers. He took a large gulp, and then another, looking at her, suddenly realising he could think of nothing prolific to say, almost uncomfortably he sat back down, his empty glass in his hand.

"It doesn't matter, does it?" he said looking over to her. "This facade? This show."

"You think this is all a 'show'? To what audience?"

"To *them*, Trudi. Those that couldn't wait to see me die, like those waiting to watch Cole die, and the others in 'the club': *that* audience. Those out there waiting to hear my story, they're like leeches, hyenas."

"No, they're not. It's human nature to want to know the truth. We all have that yearning to empathise with the underdog, to see a happy-ever-after situation and that's why so many people have been rooting for you. Hey, I totally get that you're going to need time to adapt, to understand everything. Rome wasn't built in a day, my friend."

Trevor couldn't sleep that night, but it was a different kind of being unable to sleep. Despite having so many reasons to rejoice, he felt flat, *and* guilty! He felt guilty because he was once again free to live his life, to do and be anything he chose while his once so-called friend would be stepping into his shoes with a much bigger burden to carry; however, unlike Trevor, Rocky wouldn't be given the death sentence. He'd receive something much less harsh because he'd sworn he hadn't seen Jonah that night and so his defence team were trying to keep it to the one murder, of Alice.

He tossed and turned all night, trying to fit all the pieces of the jigsaw puzzle into place believing that the experts were not seeing the full picture. If Rocky didn't see Jonah and hadn't killed him, or assisted in his death, then why was he dead and why had the prosecution blamed it on Trevor, because it was a fact that Jonah was dead, the very same night that Alice was murdered.

Trudi had shown him the photographs she'd printed from Jonah's camera and he'd had to turn his head away, seeing the result of her brother's barbaric act after what had been a joyous night for the two of them. He still didn't know how it came to be in his sister's possession. She was waiting to be questioned.

The angry and startled image of Rocky when he realised he'd been caught on camera plagued his thoughts. Had everything been planned, organised by

Rocky to get him away from his sister, or was it all a huge, fatal error?

He remembered walking back home that night, feeling high, now wishing he'd considered Alice more than his sister, insisting he ensured she was safely back inside her home, rather than worrying about Eva who'd deliberately locked her bedroom window after he'd asked her not to.

He knew his sister didn't approve of his friendship with Alice, even though he also knew she was very fond of Rocky. The two were alike in many ways, despite their age difference.

Why did Eva have that blessed camera, and why had she forsaken him?

43: Eva

Sixteen-year-old Eva sat confidently in the interview room in much the same fashion as countless others before her. Her mother sat in the corner whilst Matt Hansome and the interviewers settled down for the questioning. The word 'interrogation' was not mentioned.

She had been devastated to learn that Rocky had been remanded and cursed her mother repeatedly for handing over the damned camera to that silly do-gooder, Trudi! How dare her mother go prying amongst her belongings? She had no right to go trespassing into her bedroom and taking away her personal possessions.

She 'found' the camera, she explained. No, she couldn't say exactly when, and no she didn't know what was on it because she didn't know how to use it.

"But Eva, you – " Her mother tried to intervene.

"Please, Mrs. Bray, we need only Eva's answers." Anne felt reprimanded!

"You knew your brother was going out to meet Alice that night, didn't you? He made a habit of sneaking out of your bedroom window and usually you left it open for him, to climb back into, didn't you? Why did you decide to lock it then, that night of all nights?"

Eva shrugged her shoulders dismissively, "I *guessed* that's where he was heading, but he never said. The words he used were 'I'm going to see a man about a dog'. He could've been going to do a burglary at that time of night for all I knew, perhaps he broke into Jonah's place and stole his precious camera. Wouldn't surprise me if my perfect brother took those photographs and then hid it in my room."

"Wouldn't it?" The interviewer asked.

"Wouldn't it, what?" Eva frowned.

"You said it wouldn't surprise you if Trevor had stolen Jonah's camera. But how could he have possibly taken photographs of himself and Alice, and the photographs of Rocky with Alice, then hid it in your bedroom. Is that something Trevor would've done, steal something so valuable and treasured of the man he admired so much?"

Eva smirked, "The man he admired so much. He didn't *admire* him. Is that what he told you?" She laughed, too long. She sighed theatrically, "He tolerated the fool, like me, because we needed him. Rather, our mother needed him. He was like a sad puppy dog – "

"Eva! Stop it, don't use that kind of language. And don't talk about Jonah in – "

All heads turned towards Anne. "Mrs. Bray, any more interruptions and we'll have to ask you to leave. If you can't sit there in silence, you'll have to wait outside."

So she did. It was too much for Anne to hear. She picked up her handbag and marched out of the room.

Eva continued smirking, "It's true, the man lacked balls. Know what I mean? He gave our mother everything she wanted, financially and materialistically, but not romantically or physically. I don't think he had it in him, nice enough as he was, I guess."

"And you two, too. Trevor and you. He provided for all of you, I believe."

Eva nodded, "Yeah, I suppose. But we never asked him to. See, Jonah was a bit of a soft touch and our mom could wrap him round her little finger. I think we all could – and did! Did you know he never spent one single night at our house, nor my mother at his? Bit strange, wouldn't you say considering they could have been alone, together, at his place?

"And you think this is relevant?"

"Don't you? You're asking me questions about that night and how his camera suddenly came to light when that woman turned up out of the blue and my mother claims she found it in my room. Well, I don't know how it got there, so it looks like we're at a dead end."

Matt's brain cells were hammering away, trying to take in everything the girl was saying, wondering how much was true. It seemed like everyone was trying to pin the blame on another.

"Jonah was found dead outside his property, stung to death by the very bees he'd raised and loved.

Several hives smashed. Any idea how that may have happened?"

"My brother is the best person to answer that question. He was the one who shared that passion. Can't stand the things myself, nasty stingy pests."

"Who do you think Rocky is looking towards, in this picture?" Eva was shown the photograph of Rocky looking angrily towards the photographer.

"I think that's the burning question isn't it?"

44: Warden Statham and Cole Cave

John Statham had one last job to complete before Cole's execution. Everything else was set in place. The auditorium would be sprayed with a 'sea-breeze' atomiser that promised a calming aroma, light bulbs checked and replaced where necessary, offering a subdued ambience. The screens had been rigorously polished, fly blows erased, ensuring the audience had a perfect view of the man's final moments. Now Statham had the unwanted task of paying a visit to ascertain any last minute, legitimate, requests.

"Cave," he started, "when the chaplain recites his blessing, before the procedure begins, he will have to announce you by your Christian name, Cole Elijah Perkins, and not the name you chose to be called here, or indeed any of those you previously declared yourself as, do you understand?"

"Ah, Warden, 'a rose by any other name should smell as sweet', isn't that so?" He had a shooting memory of Caroline using the exact phrase when customers would get her name wrong, calling her Carolyn instead.

"I have never been defined by who I am as opposed to what I am, so why should mere words matter to me now? Aren't we all judged by the titles we're given? Who are you, Warden Statham, or rather, what are you? I understand the procedure, the rules. Your executioners have their own titles, too, and those reflect the very jobs they're paid to perform. 'Administrators' could be another way of describing them but less effective, wouldn't you agree? There's also my number, don't forget, 5216, that would be easier to carve on my tombstone. It matters not, sir. I won't be around to complain."

Warden Statham stared at him with contempt, recalling the hours he spent reading everything on the despicable, uncaring, unremorseful being in front of him, changing his alliances from ambivalence to loathing.

"Someone from the Governor's Office will of course be in attendance, and – "

"And the boy? Will he be here? I'd be sorry to know that he wasn't going to attend the festivities, being *kindred* spirits and all." Cole relished the look of confusion on the warden's face. "Brown!" He exclaimed, "you have that letter for him that I asked you to give to him. He has to be here."

"Yes. Yes, of course. He's confirmed he will be here, with that woman who visited him. He's also requested a final meeting with you first thing in the morning, you have an hour together. He's changed his name, by the way. Can't blame the guy; he needs to put everything behind him."

Cole grinned. "He changed his name? What a remarkably, astute thing to do."

There was an awkward moment of silence as the two men sat face to face, one smiling, one not.

"Oh, just one more thing, Warden. I'm sure my menu requisitions have been attended to, but did you manage to get a guitar for me? You know, so that I can sing my last song, the one I told you about? The song for my execution."

45: Eva's Visit to Rocky

The room was beginning to fill with visitors as each one displayed their joy upon seeing their loved ones sitting waiting for their arrival, their bright orange attire in contrast to the gloom of the occasion. Rocky, however, remained aloof with his hands clasped on the table when Eva entered.

"I've skipped school to come here to see you today and all you can do is glare at me? Thanks, buddy."

"I didn't ask you to come, that was your decision, so hurry up and say what you've come to say and leave."

"I'm hurt," Eva mocked. "After all I did for you."

"After all *you* did for *me*? We did it for each other, you stupid cow!"

"Erm, let me get this right. I went to Jonah's house to get his camera so we could take photographs of *my* brother with *your* sister to prove it was incest. Wasn't it you who told me that the pastor had fathered us all?? Why the hell did you rape and kill your own sister?"

"Why did *you* kill Jonah?" Rocky demanded, his voice in a conspiratorial whisper.

Eva looked shocked at his declaration, "I didn't! When I got to his house he wasn't there. I found him outside, already dead." She lowered her voice further, "Christ knows what happened, but his body was covered in his stupid bees! They were crawling out of his mouth too. It was horrible, but I managed to locate his camera, like you asked."

Rocky was shocked. He and Eva had never spoken after that night. Their deed was done, their secret safe.

"I'm being asked all sorts of questions, but don't worry, nobody knows it was me - *brother*!"

"I am *not* your brother!"

"Well," she scoffed, "biologically you are, according to you. You, me, Trevor, and Miles. Who'd've thought? And if you hadn't raped and murdered your own sister, none of this needed to happen. You wouldn't be sitting here now, would you?"

Eva rose from her chair purposefully, ready to leave but wanting to add her cutting departing statement: "You could have had a willing sister, Rock. I certainly wouldn't have cried 'rape'."

46: Cole

He strummed on the guitar slowly, feeling the strings, remembering his own lyrics and those classics written and performed by the loved and adored the world over, just as he wished he could've been. He'd always wanted to write the perfect love song, to be remembered by.

He'd written a love song for Caroline, the girl he liked years ago, but she never got to hear it.

They'd all shunned him, one way or the other, he told himself; starting from the day his brother was born, boy number two, the more important one, and his parents turned their affections on their newborn. For Cole, it was a constant stream of rejection, dismissal, and repulsion once the baby arrived.

So he turned away, erased his past in an endeavour to recreate himself. He found it liberating arriving in a different state, giving himself a new name, inventing a whole false history.

Truth to be told, nobody had a clue as to the real number of his crimes as many of his victims never came forward, the girls who were raped, bodies of his kills never found. Many of the small stores he robbed at gunpoint didn't have CCTV cameras and if the proprietors had been elderly, he didn't want to waste his ammunition. The younger ones, however, were not so fortunate as they would have been more adept at giving the police a clearer description of the perpetrator.

Ah, yes, he summarised. He'd had a good run up until finally getting caught, all thanks to the lovely Caroline. He chastised himself for not finishing her off when he had the opportunity. Caroline, his downfall. The only woman he'd ever had genuine feelings for.

He remembered telling Brown during one of their discussions that his biggest crime was falling in love and this he honestly believed was the truth because if he hadn't spared her, he would still be on the outside, living his dream.

Fate, that's what he'd called it. Fate, destiny, a preordained chance. Words so alike, events happening outside of one's control. He was fated to be in the same vicinity as Caroline again, thus causing his final destiny. One could even say it was *kismet.*

It was a hot, hot day, on Route 30 that he was taking to get to Philadelphia after Pittsburgh and he wanted to get off, find somewhere to stock up on a few supplies, a liquor store, gas. He cruised up to the forecourt to be filled up, passing his keys to the young man eager to assist. He hadn't noticed the campervan parked on the side.

He walked around the store, nonchalantly placing a few items in a wire basket, contemplating the logistics of pulling out his gun secreted in the waistband of his dirty jeans, scanning his surroundings surreptitiously.

He hadn't noticed the parked campervan but Caroline *had* spotted him as she emerged from the bathroom and the memories of seeing Foxy's dead dog hanging in her vehicle came flooding back.

She'd been grilled relentlessly about the sudden disappearance of Foxy afterwards. His beloved dog being crucified and left in her campervan. Everything had pointed to her as being culpable, yet there was nothing solid. She remembered giving names of everyone who came to the diner, the regulars, the ones who would sit alone and the one who disappeared shortly after she no longer wanted to spend time listening to his pathetic attempts to lure her into an appreciation of his song lyrics. The man who showed no concern for her grief surrounding Gwinnie. The one who left without so much as goodbye other than an insignificant half bone-shaped piece she found under the table as he left.

It wasn't much. In fact no one would have noticed anything out of the ordinary. Caroline herself hadn't given it another thought, until later, much later. As Cole paid for his breakfast in cash, leaving it on the table, a dog treat had slipped out of his pocket. It was the sort of treat one could buy anywhere. She was too busy grieving, at the time, to put two and two together.

Caroline had wondered then. Why did Cole have dog treats when he didn't own a dog? And afterwards, where had Foxy's guitar gone?

She darted back inside and locked herself in the cubicle, pulled out her phone and called 911.

47: The Day of the Execution

Earl Ryder had been bitterly disappointed at losing out on the opportunity of performing the ritual for The Caveman. Hammond was now back, and it was all up to him, a fact that relieved Cole a fraction. The last man's face he wanted to see was that repulsive slime-ball's.

Trevor had point blank refused to go back down to 'the club', the memories too stifling to endure, suggesting they meet 'upstairs'; and whilst he sat there alone waiting for Cole to appear, he had this foreboding feeling in the pit of his stomach, which he attributed to being back in this unforgiving environment.

A handcuffed, pathetic version of a man was escorted into the room by Pinkstone. Trevor rose from his seat, offering a heartfelt smile, glad to be able to, at last, come face to face with the man he'd spent so many, many months talking about everything and nothing. The condemned man laughed back at him, with an all knowingness about him, and *that*'s when it hit him! That face, that familiar little scar above his left eye… The pastor!

Trevor recoiled in absolute horror!

"Yooouuu!" He cried, over and over again, trying to keep his balance by holding on to the table in front of him. "It was you all along. I can't believe it! Somebody, please get me out of here, NOW! I don't wanna talk to this lowlife, there's been a big mistake. Oh, my God, you were our pastor, for God's sake, how could… how could… ?"

Cole raised his handcuffed hands high as if offering up a prayer. "What? And spoil the fun? You were the best part of my last years here. We finally got to 'know' each other, Son!"

Trevor tried to gather himself, to absorb what he was experiencing, staring in total disbelief at the laughing vision in front of him. He wouldn't sit back down because he knew he was going to leave immediately.

"You raped my mother and my friends' mothers. My aunt too? Is that why she disappeared without a trace? Did she do something wrong to make you get rid of her, did you?"

"Hey, hey, calm down, kid. Didn't I always tell you there was no such thing as a wrong woman? Oh dear, this isn't the kind of happy reunion I was anticipating. Hmmm, let me think? Anne's little sister… oh yes," he chuckled, "I remember her now. No, she didn't do anything wrong, why would you think that of your lovely aunt?"

Trevor sucked up with as much force as he could muster and spat in Cole's face. "I'll be sitting in the front row enjoying every minute. Rot in Hell, you phoney, sorry disgrace to the word 'pastor'."

He left, without so much as a backward glance. The room filled with an uncomfortable, tense, silence.

Cole turned his head over his shoulder to speak, wiping the spittle from his cheek, "You see that Pinkstone? No respect. Let's go. I'm ready now."

"Trudi, hi, it's me. Can you call Matthew for me, please, and tell him to cancel my name change? I'm going to continue being Trevor Carlton Brown. Call me soon. Xx"

48: Afterwards

Well, honey, we did it, and I'm so so proud of you! The book's doing incredibly well (no surprise there, hey?). What's the temperature out there in Miami today? Much better than here, I imagine. Have you got my room ready because my flight's booked, case packed (counting the days) and I'm desperate for a hug from my bestie and a large cocktail, of course!

I spoke to your mom, she's doing OK. No mention of your sister.

We didn't get all the answers we hoped for but at least we got the right ones. Life is like that. I learned that years ago.

And his song! The "Song of the Execution." It was wow, even you had to admit that. A brilliant and fitting ending to your book. What a shame he wasted that talent when you consider what he could have been.

I'm also dying to know what his farewell letter said. If you don't want to tell me, please forgive me in advance for my forthcoming efforts to prise it out of you.

That's all for now. Just get that pool bikini ready, amigo, cos I need to get bronzed!

Truly,

Trudi

49: The Truth – Three Years Earlier

It was early afternoon and Eva needed to borrow Jonah's camera for a couple of days.

It was always a pleasant stroll over to the Ray's farm and she was smiling to herself as she contemplated telling him she needed some money to buy the new boots she had set her sights on, too. He wouldn't refuse.

She counted the hives as she passed, far enough away from the proximity of the house. Twenty. The odd bee hovering around, buzzing faintly. She knew how many hives there were, but it was an unconscious habit to count them anyway.

She didn't find Jonah outside, so she walked up the wooden porch steps calling out his name, tapping lightly on his open front door.

After receiving no reply, Eva walked through the door and entered the kitchen. She noticed a pile of black and white photographs strewn across Jonah's dining table, his Canon camera in the middle, the one she had come to 'borrow'. She walked over and glanced at the subjects, many close-ups of bees, flowers, landscape views that appeared to have been taken from an upstairs window. She picked up a handful and smirked at seeing the church she attended weekly, all the people she knew, some of her, her brother and lots of their mother.

She called out again to Jonah, louder this time, but still the house remained silent.

She then sat down at the table and continued to flick through the familiarity of the black and white pictures. The pastor's car parked outside their house, the pastor leaving Rocky's house, and others'. But the pastor had been long gone, and she wondered why he had taken them. She vaguely remembered the visits from their pastor.

Turning each one over and seeing the dates written in pencil on the backs, the information meaning nothing to her.

She stood up from her seat as Jonah entered the kitchen, fastening the belt on his jeans and tucking in his shirt. He looked surprised to see Eva at his table, embarrassed that she'd caught him adjusting his clothing having just got back from the toilet and wondering what she had come for – this time.

They stared at each other in silence. "Jonah, I need to borrow your camera for a couple of days."

Jonah said nothing as he quickly gathered up all the photographs and placed them back in the box.

"And I need twenty dollars to get myself a new pair of boots. Look at these," she said, showing him a perfectly good sole, "they're on their last legs." She laughed sarcastically at her attempt to crack a joke.

"You are not having the camera, Eva. It's not a toy and I don't want you taking it away. I'm happy to help you with anything for your studies but it's too precious an item to let you use without my supervision. So, no to the camera. Now show me your boots again. There doesn't appear to be anything wrong with those you're wearing now."

"Oh, come on Jonah, for goodness' sake! Do we really have to go through this charade every time I ask for the slightest little thing? I don't think my mother will be pleased."

Jonah was furious. He didn't like Eva one little bit. She was a scheming, lying little madam but felt powerless to do anything other than comply to her blackmailing demands. Who would believe him against the stories of a teenage girl?

He had tried his very best with both of Anne's children over the years but there was something deep and dangerous with Eva that no amount of placating was ever going to be enough. He was going to call her bluff, stand up for himself, refuse to be used as a fool.

"Never a please or thank you from you is there, Eva? Well, my answer to both of your 'demands' is no. Now go away, and grow up. I'm busy."

Eva was incensed, how dare he refuse her! She ignored him, grabbed his camera and ran out of the door, jumped down the porch steps and continued running, thinking of ways she was going to make him pay for his refusal!

And it was whilst Jonah was running to catch up with her that he stumbled over the bellows that had toppled over as Eva furiously kicked it from its leaning position on one of the hives. As his heavy torso tumbled forwards, he tried to break his fall by trying to grasp a purchase on the structure of the hive.

It rocked slightly then toppled on its side, falling against the next one. It was like a dominoes' effect as one by one they crashed to the earth.

All she could do was watch in absolute horror as the bees began to swarm around his huge frame, hundreds and hundreds and hundreds. He tried desperately to swat them away, his arms flailing hopelessly, screaming out in pain and fear, and then she ran and ran and ran.

Acknowledgments

Firstly, I always like to start off by thanking my wonderful ladies who take time to read my words before submitting the final manuscript to my publisher. Always, my amazing 92-year-old mother – Elizabeth Talbott, and the wonderful Susan Bond who checks and double checks my numerous typos. Debbie Frearson, Pat White, Sue Robins, for their invaluable opinions and input, too.

Andrew Hartshorn is an old and very dear friend of mine and is the creator of my front cover (*Image(s) used under license from Shutterstock.com*.) I wanted him to create Trevor and gave him a few brief details to work with. But I changed my mind several times and Andrew, never sighing with exasperation, continued to work until I gave him the green light. To me, he has interpreted my requirements with the utmost precision. Thank you, Andrew Hartshorn!

Another gush of thanks go once more to Mike Hurd of Lineage Independent Publishing. Without his invaluable magic to get my scribblings published, my manuscripts would remain at the back of a drawer, never to see the light of day. I am deeply indebted to you, Mike, as always.

I would also like to finally add that in all of my books, I try to name certain characters after friends or family. Sometimes the whole name – *with their permission of course* – and others just using one name. I'm sure most writers do the same. It is my way of giving them the nod that they are in my thoughts and hopefully they recognise it is intended as a compliment.

Other Books by Lisa Talbott

Poetry and Short Stories:

Pen and Inks

Weep and Wail
(with Michael Paul Hurd)

Novels:

Spud (everything is meant to be)

A Patch of Yellow

My Name is Margot

The Liquorice Tree